LONE WOLF

Metro City

JT Fader

Published by Steambath Press

Paperback published March 2024
ISBN-13: 978-1-998008-54-4

Chapter One | Mason

The hot water felt good on my aching body. Washed away the scent of another night spent having my needs met. My aromatic soap was necessary to cover up whatever residual smell the human I had been fucked by had left on me. My carrier was right, humans smelled like rotting vegetation. Not that it stopped me from inviting them into my bed and spending a few hours on and off during the night or day swearing and grunting and making each other cum.

Because that was the goal—and nothing more.

I hadn't been in a relationship in years, and I wasn't about to start now. I'd learned my lesson. The world was a cruel place. Trusting a mate to always treat you with love led to heartache.

I shut off the water, grabbed a towel, and dried myself. I swiped my hand across the mirror so I could see myself. My eyes looked bleary and red. I hadn't been sleeping lately.

I ran my hand through my hair. Who was I kidding? I hadn't slept properly my entire life. Being the second male, third born of a mass of twelve pups had accustomed me to chaos. During the first half of my life, my siblings had stolen away the serene life I needed to sleep. I'd become accustomed to the noise, so for the second half of my life, I had trouble sleeping if it was too quiet. I'd found ways to work around my brain to get some rest.

Those late nights listening to my siblings talking seemed like a distant dream. My childhood had been filled with love and adventure. I should be better adjusted than I was.

I moved away from my home in Creekside Township twelve years ago and secured a Criminal Law and Protection degree at Metro City University. I liked order and obedience.

I smirked as I spritzed some cologne on my chest.

Especially *my* obedience. That's why I was so sore. The human had trussed me up with ropes and handcuffs and attached me to my bed. He'd used me until I'd almost tapped out.

But Mason Black wasn't a quitter.

I wandered into my bedroom naked. The muscle-bound human was asleep, his mouth open, snoring—his soft cock nestled on his hairy balls, the sheet draped across his thighs.

I exhaled.

I had told him he couldn't sleep here. No one ever slept over. My home was my sanctuary. It was the only place I could quell the feelings of being on the edge of breaking down.

I approached and nudged him.

"Hey ... buddy." I couldn't remember his name. Not sure he had told me. He simply went by @wolfmaster2409 on the app I found him on. There was an entire culture out there in the gay world, human males who specialized in pleasuring male wolves who liked to submit.

I hated that it was considered a kink. At least to the humans. To some of us wolves, it was a necessity. I attributed the need to an outright ban on shifting and hunting within city limits. We had no outlet to calm our inner wolf. Submission worked. Hence, the *kink* was in demand.

I shoved him, jostling him. He grunted and opened his eyes.

I crossed my arms. "You can't stay here."

"Thought we could have another go around."

"I've showered."

"You can have another shower."

"I don't want to have another one. I'm tired. You need to go."

"Fine." The human rolled and swung his feet out of my bed. He was slow to continue but he eventually rose to his feet. He reached out to stroke my face, but I jerked away.

Intimate touches in bed were the only ones allowed.

I didn't go for that affectionate stuff.

"Asshole," he muttered beneath his breath. "You weren't even that good."

"At what? Lying still as you fucked me senseless? Kinda hard to mess that up. Couldn't have been my lack of vocalization. *You* gagged me as soon as we arrived in the bedroom."

"Like I said … asshole. That's all you were."

"Fine." I picked up each piece of his clothing and thrust it all at him. "Out."

He clung to everything and headed for the living room. I decided to let him dress before kicking him out. Mrs. Johnson didn't need to inadvertently see a naked man in the hallway.

Again.

Turns out Mrs. Johnson is like me. She doesn't sleep much. And tends to wander the halls in the middle of the night. At eighty-six, she probably doesn't need much sleep. Or, at least, that's what I've heard about older humans. My aged sire, not so much. He can sleep for ages, especially now that he isn't the leader of the East Creekside pack anymore, my eldest brother, Maddox, having taken over a few years ago. My sire and his fated mate had stepped down.

Lucas and Adam Black—a love story for the ages.

Hence the twelve pups.

The human had to carry his boots into the hallway to put on. I couldn't stand his scent any longer. He must be one of those vegetarians. The smell of soybeans was distinct.

The putrid aroma had transferred to his spunk.

I had been extra vigilant with my after-sex douching routine.

As I headed back to the bedroom, my cell phone rang.

Now what?

The phone number of my sergeant displayed on the screen. I briefly considered not answering it. I knew better than to do that. They were taking a chance on me. I was one of the youngest detectives the Metro City police department had ever employed.

I'd excelled as a police officer.

Someone had noticed.

Either that or the department was trying to bolster the number of wolves they had in the role of detective. A minority hire. I didn't care. I'd been given an opportunity to prove myself.

If my broody, obnoxious personality didn't get me fired first.

"Detective Black," I answered.

"Black. Sorry to wake you."

"I was up. What's happened?"

"We have a 187."

Murder. What's new? This was Metro City. We were breaking records if we had less than two murders a night. Why was my sergeant phoning me? The lead detective should be calling.

"I want you to take the lead on it," my sergeant added, answering my question.

Sergeant Baker. Big Al Baker to those who knew him well. I was a long way from being able to call him that. I was a thorn in his side. He was usually yelling at me for insubordination.

I had a problem.

My sire called it a chip on my shoulder the size of Mount Everest. I called it defending myself in a world where most wolves were larger than me. Even for an Omega, I was *lean*.

On the positive side, I was easy to toss around in bed.

"Are you sure?" I asked. "I haven't covered many murder cases yet."

"Says in your files, you've attended twenty-six. Worked as second in command in eleven."

True.

Maybe I was ready. We hadn't managed to solve even half of those cases, but I'd put in some good work. Been praised for it. My performance had soothed the sergeant's opinion of me—somewhat. That much was evident by the fact he was trusting me to take the lead on a case.

I knew the procedure and the lines of inquiry that needed to be made. Knew what to look for when it came to the murder scene and the suspects. I'd been told I had a keen eye for detail. Taking the lead, I'd be required to employ every sense I had.

"What's the address?"

"The Grand Metro. Room 1410."

"Be there in 15."

I hung up the phone and looked around my living room for the white button-up shirt and grey suit I had shed when my *guest* arrived. I'd been conscientious and draped everything over a chair. The chair's fabric didn't match the sofa occupying most of the space. My two-bedroom apartment was neat but modest, a remnant of my officer days. Maybe I could upgrade soon.

After dressing, I checked myself in the mirror in my front entry. I hated that I bordered on pretty. My carrier told me my feminine looks took after his carrier's side of the family.

Both of my protectors, what humans called *parents*, were attractive, but unlike me, they were on the large side, especially my carrier. He was big for an Omega male. Muscular and built.

Not sure were I got the smaller stature from, but my Uncle Jonas was like me, including the black hair. It had to be in our genes somewhere. We were considered delicate for wolves.

I scooped my keys off the table below the mirror. My tie was straight, and I looked presentable. That's all that mattered. The evidence I had been tied up an hour before and still bore the marks from the ropes was hidden beneath my clothes.

I took the elevator to the underground parking lot and clicked the unlock button on my key fob for my car. There was no sound. I needed a new car. I was still driving around a gasoline-powered model from the dark ages. Now that I had a detective's salary, I'd been saving up.

The current classic car was my baby, but her appeal was fading.

My sire had offered to buy me a brand-new electric car, but I'd refused. He was proud of me, and I appreciated him, and his support of my dreams, but I was an adult.

I could buy my own car.

I opened my driver's door with my key—like a caveman.

The sky had opened up three days ago, pouring down torrential rain. It wasn't forecast to let up for at least a week. One thing you could say about Metro City; the weather left a lot to be desired. 302 days of rain a year. It added to the dreary ambiance of the city.

My wipers couldn't even keep up, but I knew my way around these dark streets. Grid upon grid of skyscrapers lit by neon pink and blue advertisements for the latest drink, cigarette, or other vice. Some of the buildings had video screens four stories high with glamorous women displayed, trying to convince you to invest in the latest health trend in contradiction to the cigarette ads. Metro City was a consumer mecca. Health products and vices went hand in hand.

Fuck.

I slammed on my brakes as a soaking wet human and their shopping cart crossed the street. There were a lot of homeless people in the city. Homelessness and drugs were rampant.

The city needed to do better. I was doing my small part by working for the police department, trying to keep murderers and thieves off the streets. I knew it wasn't enough.

Around the corner, the aroma of Asian street food wafted in through the back window on my driver's side that wouldn't quite close. The smell of food reminded me I hadn't fed in days.

My choices were slim. Beef, beef, and more beef with the occasional hock of pork if my funds were running low. At home, I'd grown up on venison from the surrounding forest. Now, I would have to drive for two hours to hunt for my own game. Venison and boar were an unattainable delicacy. I steered my way through a string of puddles and potholes.

I pulled up outside the Grand Metro. The circular driveway out front of the upscale hotel looked like a rave with flashing red and blue lights of at least ten police cruisers.

This was serious. Usually, we didn't see even half of that number attend.

I found an empty spot for my car among the sea of strobing lights, and dashed through the pelting rain, using the collar on my raincoat as protection for my head. Despite my best efforts, water dripped off the tip of my nose as I stepped through the glass revolving doors.

I approached the line of police officers blocking the elevators and showed my identification card and badge. There was some discussion before they let me pass.

An elevator was waiting.

I punched the button for the fourteenth floor. I smirked. There was no thirteenth floor. Humans were strange. Most of their superstitions were without foundation.

The elevator door opened to a buzz of activity.

First order of business, all the police officers, except for those who first attended, needed to go. This wasn't an opportunity to be common looky-loos.

I shoved my way to the door of suite 1410, turned, and held up both hands.

"Shut it!" I shouted. "If you weren't first to attend, get the hell out of here! This is a fucking crime scene not a freak show at a carnival! Go find something else to do—like your jobs!"

There were a few grumbles, but the hallway cleared, the elevator crammed a few times. I calmed my mind and turned on my senses. I discounted the scent of my cologne. If I'd known I would be coming to a murder scene, I never would have worn any.

Other than the victim, I was one of two wolves here. The other was a Beta female. I touched the damaged door frame. The metal door had been breached with some force. It looked like the work of one of our department's entry tools. The door must have been locked.

But why the need to bust it open?

I slipped on a pair of standard-issue blue paper booties over my shoes.

The inside of the suite was crowded with people too but from what I could tell, they were all essential—for now. Two officers, two first responders, and a forensic tech.

Most were jammed into the small bathroom. I inhaled before I approached the crime scene and attempted to catalog what I was picking up. Some scents were clear and definable, but there were a variety of indistinct smells in the small space of the hotel suite.

"Everyone out of the bathroom except forensics," I said above the hum of voices. The word had been passed around that I was taking the lead on this case. People moved out of my way.

Jeezus.

I squatted near the bathtub, ensuring I didn't touch anything. Reclined in the tub, his eyes staring blindly at the ceiling, was a male Alpha wolf. A big muscular one. From one ear to the other, his throat was slit open, exposing his trachea. The tub contained melting ice cubes.

They possessed a pink hue among rivulets of washed-out crimson.

His throat and chest were coated in a thick bib of blood.

Some arterial spray on the tiles and the partially closed shower curtain. None on the floor.

His knees bent to accommodate his size in the tub.

He appeared to be naked. The part of him I could see anyway. The ice was to the bottom of his ribcage. I could barely make out the dark outline of what looked to be his bare cock.

Had the filling of the tub with ice been interrupted?

He'd been drinking scotch and there was a faint scent of cum.

His.

I couldn't see the weapon that had been used to open his throat.

Perhaps beneath the ice.

Why ice?

To throw us off how long he'd been dead?
No.
Hypothermia causes decreased blood flow.
The goal was to slow blood loss.

I checked the tub edge and floor. I'd scanned the countertop and sink on entry.

No signs of a struggle.

Did he do this to himself?

Back to no visible weapon. There was no fur in the tub. He hadn't partially shifted and used a claw to open his throat and allowed his body to shift back out of wolf form.

"Was the light on like this?" I asked no one in particular.

"No, it was off," someone replied.

"Who found him?"

One of the officers standing in the doorway answered.

"We found him. The hotel staff called us. There were complaints of excessive noise from the ice machine in the hallway. Took them a while to investigate it—a busy night for noise. They found a few dropped ice cubes outside his door. Assumed this suite was the culprit."

I turned to look at the officer. "Why were *we* called?"

"Hotel staff reported that when they knocked on the door to ask the guest to stop using the ice machine, they heard the sound of the sliding glass door slam—then glass breaking."

I'd come back to that.

"Any name yet?"

"Hotel staff is looking into it. It doesn't appear anyone officially checked in."

I rose to my feet and pushed my way into the main room. Sure enough, someone had slammed the sliding glass door hard enough that the glass had broken.

Leading to the door, a trail of particles of soil. The dirt smelled wet and earthy with a hint of cow manure. The diminishing trail of it went from the sliding door to the bed to the entry door and the bathroom. Someone had been walking around in here with dirty shoes.

"How long did it take you to attend?" I asked.

"Hotel staff phoned right away when they couldn't gain entry. We were here in 10 minutes."

Strange.

"How come the hotel staff couldn't get in?" I asked.

"That little metal thingy." The officer pointed at the door. "The extra security feature. It was latched over. The door couldn't be opened with a key card alone."

I looked out onto the balcony—if you could call it that. There wasn't even enough depth for it to hold a chair. The wide door was meant to allow abundant airflow into the room. The hotel must have been built before the city became overcrowded and the back alleys and streets were filled with pungent garbage. There was no such thing as fresh air in Metro City anymore.

The city might have been beautiful once. Now it was a cesspool.

A stinking cesspool I loved.

I came from fresh air and open spaces, but I felt more at home here. All the noise, pollution, and cramped streets drowned out the commotion and destructive memories in my head.

I would get my fill of the pulse of the city then head back to my apartment where I could decompress. The more fucked up my day was, the more likely it was I could sleep.

I was messed up. I knew that.

It wasn't my protectors' fault. I'd been born broken. They had given us pups everything they could to secure our happiness and well-being. They were amazing *parents*.

I simply wasn't like my siblings. They were all happy and well-adjusted. After 16 years with them, I needed to be surrounded by chaos to find solitude.

My parents had been devastated when I left home at sixteen, mere days after I shifted for the first time. The celebration of my shifting had been the only time I had ever hunted.

I'd never shifted again other than the few times my previous mate had insisted on it as a form of foreplay. Wrestling, tumbling, snarling, and growling tended to turn him on.

Among other things.

I pulled a flashlight from my coat pocket and shone it on the floor of the balcony. There were clumps of damp earth and pieces of moss beneath the broken glass. Atop everything, a few small white feathers, and green droppings. Damned pigeons had contaminated the scene.

I wrinkled my nose.

Musty.

"Can you check his shoes?" I asked the officer. "See if there's any mud on them."

"No can do."

I turned and shone the light on his face. "Why not?"

"There aren't any. No clothes of any kind in the room. Not even a suitcase."

I turned back toward the balcony, placed my foot on the guide rail on the floor, and peered out. The next balcony over was at least twelve feet away. The same distance in the other direction. We'd need to check the bushes fourteen stories below this balcony for his clothes.

I scanned the room. The emergency attendants weren't needed anymore. The guy was dead. There was no disputing that. Not sure why they were sticking around.

"Hey." I snapped my fingers until one of them turned around. "Yeah, you. You and your buddy can leave now. I think we've established there's no bringing this guy back."

The coroner could arrange to transport the body to the morgue.

I returned my attention to the attending officer.

"Have you talked to the neighbors on either side?"

The officer brought out his electronic notepad and tapped the screen. "Cathy and Mitchell Dunnigan." He pointed toward the right side of the room. "They were the ones who complained about the ice machine being used repeatedly."

"Is that all they heard?" I asked.

"They remember hearing a muffled conversation before the ice machine fiasco started."

"So, our victim might have been in here with someone earlier in the night." Or it could have been his television. "What about the neighbors on the other side, and above and below?"

"Upstairs and downstairs didn't hear anything. Other side, the same as the Dunnigans. Except, the ice machine woke them. They turned on their television to drown out the sound."

"No one looked in the hallway to see who was making all the noise?"

"Nope. One side called hotel staff. The other figured it was none of their business."

They were a place to start. "I want to find out everything about the people closest to this suite. Once we figure out who the victim is, I want to know if there's any overlap in their lives. Personal disagreement. Work rival. A recent traffic accident between them. Anything."

The officer tapped away on his screen, making notes. It looked tedious. I was lucky. I had a mind like a steel trap. I made allowances for others by displaying the facts and findings on a board in the bull pen, but the details of every case were locked in my brain.

I rarely wrote anything down.

I surveyed the room. On the dining table was a bottle of scotch and one glass. I stepped closer and shone my flashlight on the table. There was a faint outline of the bottom of a glass on its surface. Either our victim had set his glass down in two separate places or there was another glass. I bent forward and sniffed the glass. The victim, scotch, and a subtle chemical smell.

The last scent was unfamiliar.

"I want this room torn apart by forensics. I think there's a second glass in here somewhere."

"You think he shared a drink with his killer?"

We weren't even sure this was a murder. All options open. I didn't want to miss anything. This was my first case, and I was going to solve it. Buck the trend for murder convictions in the city. "It's a possibility. If we find prints and DNA, this could be an easy one."

"Speaking of prints …." The forensic tech walked toward me. Pretty sure her name was Daisy. I'd only met her once before. Wrote her off because she's so young.

Like eight years younger than me young. I was young for a detective at twenty-eight. She looked like she was a teenager. She must have been one of those wolf prodigies who went to university before she even shifted back to wolf-form for the first time.

The fact she was a wolf didn't enamor her to me. Being my species wasn't a free pass. It was the same with who I invited into my bed. I didn't have an affinity for humans or wolves in or out of my bedroom. In the bedroom, wolves and humans had to follow the same set of rules.

I liked to be dominated but not left with marks. I had limits. No kissing. And no touching me once off the bed. I wasn't looking for a relationship or repeats.

As for personal friendships, wolf, or human, I didn't have any.

Plain and simple.

I preferred to be alone.

"Did you find some prints?"

Daisy huffed out a laugh. "That's the thing … the victim … no prints."

I followed her to the bathroom where she used a gloved hand to lift one of the victim's arms, holding the hand for me to look at. She was right, the wolf didn't appear to have fingerprints.

"How could this happen?" I asked.

"Well, either he was born without them, or he had them removed."

"You can do that?"

Daisy brushed her thumb across the victim's. "If he did, he did a pretty smooth job. You'd expect to see scarring from the chemicals one would use to remove them."

"So, likely born that way."

"That would be my guess."

"Are you able to determine how long he's been dead?"

"That's difficult because of the ice."

I studied the victim's face. Despite his lack of color, he was a handsome wolf. I followed the suicide thread. He shared a late-night drink with someone. Maybe more. Saw them out, filled the tub with ice, and locked the door. When the hotel staff knocked, he pitched his clothes over the balcony, slammed the sliding glass door, immersed himself in the ice, and slit his throat.

Our quick response wouldn't have left enough time for slow blood loss.

And where was the blade?

I stared closer at his face.

He looked familiar.

"Detective." The second officer leaned through the door. "They found the murder weapon."

I strode back into the main room. "Where?"

"Just under the bed—there." He pointed at the edge of the bed nearest the window. More forensic techs had arrived and were combing through the room. The space was becoming a landscape of tented evidence markers, fingerprint powder, and luminol.

A tech handed me a plastic evidence bag. Inside was a bloody utility knife. My theory of possible suicide went out the window. There was no way the wolf could have slit his throat in the main room and made it to the bathroom to immerse himself in the bathtub of ice.

There would be blood all over the carpet.

There was none.

"Are there fingerprints on the knife?"

A tech took the bag back from me. "You'll have to wait until we're done in the lab."

"Smudges, then. Anything?"

"It looks wiped clean."

It didn't make sense. Why had the murderer taken the victim's clothes but not the murder weapon? Why leave it for us to find? And how had the murderer escaped the room?

"I need to get up to the roof."

I turned and bumped straight into a human who hadn't been in the room a second ago. My nostrils were so filled with the scent of blood, that I hadn't detected him arriving.

I inhaled as I looked him up and down. Even with his scent obscured by blood, I should have heard him enter the room. The guy was built like a wall.

A seductive-looking wall who filled out a suit nicely.

I was intrigued.

At his belt line, a detective's badge.

For fuck's sake.

I shoved past him. I didn't have time for this. The human kept pace with me as I took off into the hallway, ditching my booties, and searching for someone from the hotel staff.

"Who are you?" I barked at him, annoyed that it appeared I had been assigned a parasite.

"Detective Jones."

"And what is Detective Jones going to do for me?"

The detective joined me in the elevator. "I'm here to assist you."

"I never requested a second in command." It was my choice whether I wanted to work with another detective. Most detectives managed fine by coordinating with officers.

"Sergeant Baker thought you could make use of me."

I leaned against the mirrored wall of the elevator and looked him over. I could *make use* of him, all right. He was a strapping, young human male, likely a couple of years younger than me. He had lean fingers twitching nervously. He was probably good with his hands.

Okay. I could play the game.

"We need the keys to the roof," I told him. "Think you can do that?"

The elevator opened on the main floor. I let Detective Jones step out, pretended to follow him, but then stepped back. "Get the keys. I'll meet you up there."

I chuckled at his expression as the doors closed; his mouth popping open and closed like a goldfish. He'd obviously been told by Sergeant Baker that he wasn't to let me out of his sight.

Despite the overwhelming brutality of the murder and my professionalism ...

... this development was going to be fun.

Chapter Two | Arnie

The elevator door slid across and closed, shuttering the smirk on Detective Black's face. Two minutes on the job and I'd failed at my assigned objective.

I knew my mouth was hanging open, but I was having trouble recovering enough to close it. Despite all the warnings, the covert move had been unexpected.

Sergeant Baker had told me Detective Black was a handful. That's why I had been assigned to watch him. By all accounts, Black had a brilliant analytical mind, which is why the sergeant had decided to give him his own case. The department needed a win in the category of solved cases. The mayor was breathing down the sergeant's neck.

He'd decided to take a chance on Black.

I closed my mouth and looked toward the front desk. I'd been tasked with getting the keys to the roof of the hotel. If I was lucky, Black would be waiting up there for me when I took the stairs to the roof. It made sense that he wanted to check it out. Access to the room was in question. I leaned against the desk and cleared my throat to get the concierge's attention.

"Hey, I'm Detective Jones." I flashed him my badge. "I need the keys to the roof."

The man furrowed his brow at me. "No one is allowed up there."

"I understand. I'm sure that's usually the case, but we're conducting a murder investigation. We need to check the roof above the victim's room. We need to find out if—"

I stopped myself from saying more. I had a habit of talking too much. Especially when I was nervous. I had recently embarked on a quest for self-improvement. Top problem—talking too much. If I was to have any success when it came to working on myself, I needed to master that.

"I have to speak to the manager," the concierge said.

"That's fine. I'll wait."

I leaned my back against the counter as the concierge went into a side room. The police were only maintaining a minor presence. It was doubtful the murderer was still on the premises. Especially since the door of the suite had been secured with a safety device that could only be flipped in place from inside the suite. An officer in the hallway had filled me in when I arrived.

The killer had somehow escaped from off the balcony.

My mind wandered.

The dim lights of the bedside table lamps had been replaced by forensic lights by the time I got to the suite. Even in the harsh light, Detective Black's appearance had caught me by surprise.

I adjusted my collar as I waited, flustered by my experience with him. His short, jet-black hair and delicate features, ivory skin the color of summer clouds, and rose-colored lips were stunning. If the sergeant hadn't told me Detective Black was a wolf, I never would have guessed.

He was certainly living up to his reputation of being difficult to work with.

"The manager says you can have the keys."

I turned back to face the desk and held out my hand to receive the keys from the reluctant-looking concierge. Not sure what his problem was with us going on the roof. I added him to our list of potential suspects in my head and snapped my hand closed on the keys. "Thank you."

Walking back across the entry to the elevators, the grey marble floors amplified every sound. A woman in stilettos joined me in the cramped, square metal box with canned musac.

"What floor?" I asked her.

"Six."

I pushed the button for the sixth floor, and set my stance, trying to look professional. I would push the button for the top floor once she exited the elevator. I didn't want her to know where I was going. For all I knew, she was a reporter looking for a scoop on what was happening with the investigation. Word was probably out there already—that there had been a gruesome murder in the most expensive hotel in the city. Crimes against rich people always drew attention.

I nodded at her as she stepped past me and off the elevator. She hadn't given me a second look for the entire trip to her floor. Not sure why I bothered to be interested in women. They were rarely attracted to me. I had quite an impressive stature, but my face was nothing special.

I was plain compared to someone like Detective Black.

He probably had no trouble finding women.

I'd noticed he didn't wear a wedding band. I knew it was a human custom, but some wolves had started doing it; having a wedding to say their vows to their chosen or fated mate in front of friends and family. Maybe Detective Black hadn't found his mate yet.

I didn't understand the wolves' mating structure. The idea of finding someone you're fated to be with and being unable to resist them—and *mating* with them as soon as you met them …?

Then instantly committing to spend the rest of their lives together.

It boggled the mind.

The numbered light above the button panel displayed that I had reached the 24th floor.

Another six floors to go.

Detective Black better be waiting for me.

The elevator opened onto a hallway that looked exactly like the fourteenth floor. I walked to the end and found the door leading to a set of stairs that would take me to the roof.

I exhaled a sigh of relief. Detective Black was sitting at the top of the concrete steps. He was tapping away on his phone, the light illuminating his alluring face in the darkness.

I flicked on the overhead light.

Detective Black lifted his head, squinting at me. He tucked his phone in his pocket. I had likely interrupted something personal. The sergeant had told me the detective didn't take notes.

Keeping notes was part of my duties in assisting.

"Detective," I said. "I have the keys."

"Good boy."

I cringed. Detective Black wasn't that much older than me. Sure, I was young and had been fast-tracked. One of the perks of being Sergeant Baker's nephew.

I refused to be talked down to.

"Please, call me Jones."

Detective Black stood with his hands in his pockets and studied me. "Call me Black."

I took a few steps up the stairs. "Let's get onto the roof."

"Give me the keys." Black held out his hand. I walked closer and handed the keys over.

It took a bit of effort, but Black finally opened the door. I wrapped my coat tighter around myself and stepped into the downpour of cold rain. Black went straight to the very edge of the roof and started taking measured steps back along the flat gravel surface. He stopped and looked back. He seemed satisfied that we were above the correct set of balconies.

I joined him at the edge of the expanse. There was a three-foot wall with crumbling capstones surrounding the entire roof. He squatted to examine a capstone. Some of the moss that covered the rest of the capstones was missing from the one in front of us. I fished my electronic notepad out of my pocket and took a picture of the groove through the spongey plant material.

Black shifted backward and looked at the gravel. He made a grunting noise. He wasn't pleased with what he was finding. "There's very little soil up here," he said.

"Were you expecting to find more?"

"It had to come from somewhere."

Black lifted what soil there was and sniffed it. "It's the same as in the suite." I made a note of that. I had never worked with a wolf before. Their heightened senses were definitely an asset.

"Collect some of it," he said.

"Right. Okay." I tucked the notepad back in my pocket and retrieved an evidence bag. I was practically down on my knees collecting a sample when I heard the door to the roof shut. We had propped it open with a brick. There was no handle on the roof side.

He'd locked me on the roof.

"Fuck!"

I sprang back to my feet and closed the bag containing the small amount of soil. I didn't have the number for any of the officers attending the scene to come retrieve me off the roof.

"Asshole."

I fished my phone out of my pocket, swallowed my pride, and phoned dispatch.

"Metro City dispatch."

"Hey, it's Detective Jones. I'm attending the Grand Metro murder and I've inadvertently locked myself on the roof. Can you call someone on-site to come and let me down?"

The female dispatcher snickered. "You did what?"

"Locked myself on the roof." There was no way I was telling anyone my new boss and partner had pulled a fast one and made a fool of me.

Dispatch sighed after laughing for much longer than I thought was professional. "I'll send someone up to let you in."

I closed the call and started pacing the roof. To make myself useful, I searched the roof for somewhere a rope could have been tied off. There was a metal pipe that looked secure enough.

Black had probably already made note of it.

I groaned as I made another circuit of the roof. This blunder was going to be the topic of department jokes for some time. I needed to be more aware when it came to Black.

Sure enough, the officer who popped open the door was already laughing.

"How on earth …?" He held the door as I burst past him.

"The wind blew the door closed."

"That wind wouldn't happen to be named Black, would it?"

I jogged down the stairs. "Maybe."

"Jones, listen. Black told me to come get you before I got the call from dispatch. He might be difficult to work with, but he would never compromise a case. He's just messing with you."

"I'll try to keep that in mind as I'm watching my back."

"While you're doing that … pay attention. You're young. You'll learn something from him."

"He's not that much older than me."

"Yeah, but his mind … scary. He's been instrumental in solving a lot of cases."

"Where is he now?"

"Last I saw him; he was headed to the main floor to check out the landscaping below the balcony of the victim. I'd hurry if I was you. Not sure he'll be there for long."

I dashed for the elevator, leaving the officer behind. He didn't seem particularly interested in catching up to me, instead, standing in the hallway and checking his notepad. It felt as if it took forever for the elevator to reach my floor and then descend to the lobby.

I hustled, my wet worn dress shoes slipping as I crossed the lobby floor and pushed through a backdoor. I spotted Black's head above some bushes out the rear of the hotel.

He motioned me over.

"No clothes, but I found footprints," he said as I joined him. He flashed his light at the ground. Sure enough, there was a trail of footprints leading from the walkway to a spot directly beneath the row of balconies. Boots. And then they just stopped.

I scanned around, following his light.

There were no more.

"See how the toes of the last set of prints dig into the soil?" He nudged me. "Take a picture. I'll call forensics down here to process the area."

I did as he asked but kept one eye on him. He didn't appear to be contemplating taking off on me again. Maybe we were past that game.

"It'll take a while for the evidence to be processed," he said. "I can formulate a plan of investigation from home. Might be best if you get some sleep. I can be difficult to keep up with."

"I'll be fine. I can go in early and start setting up the board."

"Whatever works for you and the team is fine by me."

"Do you really never take notes?"

"I can't write as fast as I think. It would slow me down." He tapped his head. "It's all up here."

I gave him a quizzical look. Now I was concerned. Black wasn't the only one who needed access to that information. The whole team would need to examine it.

He patted my shoulder. "Don't worry, Jones. Everything that's rattling around in my brain ends up on the computer to add to the file. I'm not arrogant enough to work in a bubble."

Black stepped away from the prints and wove his way through the bushes. He was on his phone to forensics when I exited the landscaping. I shook my hands and wiped my face.

I was soaked through from the rain.

"Do you need a ride home?" Black asked.

"Actually, I do." I had hitched a ride with an officer who was kind enough to take pity on me and my current situation of having my car in for repair.

"My car is out front."

I followed Black through the lobby and back into the rain. We approached a car that had seen better days. It appeared to be an old gas-powered model. They were a rarity to see.

"Interesting car," I said.

"Don't start. It's a collector's model."

From what century? I opened the passenger door, climbed in, and pulled and latched my seatbelt. I couldn't wipe the smirk off my face. Even I had a better car.

With my door closed, I inhaled the earthy scent of Black's cologne. I hadn't noticed it up on the roof. For some reason, it humanized him. A wolf wearing cologne—amplified my smirk.

"What's your address?"

"I'm in *The Towers*." It was usually a shock to most people that I lived in city housing, but I hadn't lived an easy life. I grew up in housing. Spent some time in foster care. I'd been raised by a single mom who had trouble keeping a job. She had the disease of addiction. There were stretches of days at a time when I'd been forced to fend for myself at a very young age.

When my mom passed away, I kept the apartment. The rent was cheap, and I was used to the place. Being a member of the police force brought some grief down on my head, though. Some of my neighbors weren't exactly law-abiding citizens. Many of them, I'd grown up with.

"Rough neighborhood," Black commented as he fired up his noisy combustion engine.

"I'm used to it."

"You lived there for long?"

"My whole life."

"Huh." Black eased his car onto the street.

"What does *huh* mean?"

"I just find it strange. You've shot up through the ranks even faster than me. Which means only one thing. You know someone. I'm going to guess the sergeant."

"That's an arrogant statement."

"I've never been accused of being humble."

I grunted. "Are you saying the *only* reason I'm here is because I know someone?"

Black took a corner way too fast. My shoulder hit the door.

Pretty sure he did it on purpose.

"No," he replied. "I'm sure you have other merits."

"Top of my class."

"So was I. Valedictorian. So what?"

I huffed and crossed my arms. "Fine. Sergeant Baker is my uncle."

"Then I'm back to *huh*. Why *The Towers*? Sergeant is a guy of means."

I angled my body, so I had a better view of Black; the light and dark of the streetlights like ivory and black piano keys dragging across his features. The effect was mesmerizing.

"Figure it out," I said, challenging him.

"Your suit is new, so this is a recent post for you, but it's off the rack, untailored, which means money is a problem. And your shoes are old. At least five years out of date."

"Okay, so I don't have the best clothes."

"You weren't expecting to get the post so soon. The monetary outlay caught you off guard."

True.

"You were too proud to ask your uncle for funds."

Again—true.

"Your ears are pierced in six places."

I touched one earlobe. How the hell had he noticed that? "I had a rebellious phase."

"You have a thin finger of a crimson tattoo visible above your shirt collar." He tapped his fingers on his steering wheel. "Crimson Dragons? Their gang is prevalent in your area."

My jaw shifted back and forth of its own accord. He was going to do it. Black was going to break down my entire life after only knowing me for an hour.

"Gang life. You had very little supervision growing up. And even though you were in a gang, you're even-tempered and well-spoken. A woman's influence. Dad was out of the picture."

We pulled into the parking lot of *The Towers*.

He continued.

"Sergeant Baker wasn't aware how bad things were because his sister kept it from him. Otherwise, he would have helped you sooner." Black turned and looked at me. "Drug problem?"

Impossible. No one was that observant.

Except, maybe a wolf.

"You're frightening, you know that?"

"I've been told."

"I'm going to get out now," I said.

"Not stopping you."

"Wasn't sure if you were finished analyzing me."

"You're a meat eater. Primarily beef. And you prefer natural soap and shampoo."

"Enough." I unlatched my seatbelt and pushed open the car door.

"You have a cat. Wait—no. Two cats."

I could hear him chuckling as I exited the car. I couldn't stop the grin that stretched across my face. He was teasing me now. Trying to get a rise out of me. Parlor tricks.

My new boss was a wolf—and a smart ass.

He might grow on me.

I didn't look back as he pulled away. My focus was on the group of men gathered near the door of my building. I knew all of them. Two of them had been best friends of mine as a kid.

"Arnie, dude." All five men crowded around me, stopping me from reaching the door and trying to intimidate me. Wasn't going to work. I could hold my own. "Boyfriend drop you off?"

"He's my boss." I fished my keys out of my pocket.

"He's awfully pretty to be a guy."

I pressed my way between two of the men and slipped my key into the lock. "Don't say that around him. He's a wolf. Not sure he'd take too kindly to being made fun of."

One of the men scoffed. "Him? A wolf?"

I turned my key in the lock. "I'm tired. Can we continue this another time?"

"Your boss is a wolf?"

"Yeah." I hauled open the door. "So pretty sure it's not a good idea to mess with me either."

One of my old friends, Dusty, ruffled my hair. "Come on, Arnie. We're just teasing you."

"Whatever." I pushed past our neighborhood thugs and mounted the steps two at a time. They didn't follow. There would be no point. I wasn't entertaining enough. I wasn't afraid of them. I had a lot of stairs to climb. My building was ten stories high, and I was on the tenth. The stairs, although they had a door at their base, were on the exterior of the building. Once on a floor, you accessed your apartment door from a long exterior walkway. From your front door, you could see across the concourse to another building that looked exactly the same.

The welcoming committee came running as soon as I opened my door. Black had been right. I had two cats. Mittens and Carlos. They'd come to me pre-named.

I bumped the door closed with my hip and locked it. I might feel comfortable in my housing situation, but I wasn't stupid enough to leave my door unlocked.

I tossed my keys into a bowl and squatted to give the cats some loving. The sun would be coming up soon. I might be able to squeeze in a couple of hours of sleep before then.

The cats weren't keen to follow me to the bedroom. They figured I was up—they should be up. I changed out of my new suit into flannel sweatpants and a t-shirt and dried my hair with a towel. I padded into the kitchen and submitted to the yowling requests to be fed.

I dumped half a can of wet food into each of their dishes and headed back to the bedroom. If I was lucky, Mittens and Carlos would be content enough that they wouldn't bother me.

My colorful, childhood comforter welcomed me as I climbed beneath it. I cozied into the warm, enveloping space, and closed my eyes. The sound of sirens lulled me toward sleep.

My eyes popped open.

My phone was ringing.

Not again.

Being pulled from sleep once during the night was enough. I thumped about blindly with my hand, trying to find my phone on my bedside table.

I held it up to my face.

Didn't recognize the number.

"Hello?"

"Jones—it's Black."

I sat up. "I'm trying to sleep. I told you I'd see you in a few hours."

"Someone broke into my apartment."

That was unfortunate, but what did someone breaking into my boss's apartment have to do with me? "Have you phoned the station?"

"No, I phoned *you*."

I struggled out from beneath my comforter and placed my feet on the floor. I suspected this was going to require me to abandon the promise of sleep and head back into the world.

"Why did you phone me instead of the station?"

"I think the break-in is tied to our case."

I shuffled forward on my mattress, poised to stand.

"Why?"

"Just get over here. I need your help processing the scene."

"We have a forensic team for that."

"I don't want them in my apartment." A whine traveled down the line. "Please, Jones."

He was practically panting—like a wolf.

"Fine. Text me your address. I'll call a taxi. Try to breathe."

Ten minutes later, I was hurtling through the streets in my sweats, headed for the other side of town. The good side. Not the rich part of the city but certainly better than where I lived.

We pulled up outside a steel and glass skyscraper.

I looked up as I stood outside the doors. Black was on the 30th floor. He was probably right. A break-in that high in the building wasn't random. Opportunistic break-ins happened on the first few floors. The doorknob jigglers who managed to slip inside behind a resident.

I punched the code he had given me into the intercom panel.

"Jones?"

"Yup."

The glass door beside me buzzed. I pulled it open and stepped into the front entry. It had seen happier times. The furniture was worn from years of neglect, and the paint faded. It had once been a vibrant burgundy. Now it was a washed-out crimson with black scuff marks near the floor. I pressed the elevator button a few times like Black had told me to. It finally opened. Beyond the doors, a dark cavern. I had to use my phone's flashlight to select Black's floor.

The elevator shook and jumped, then started moving. I grabbed the handrail. Not sure why. It certainly wouldn't save me if the elevator decided to plummet into the basement.

I survived.

The hallway to Black's apartment was similar to the ground floor. Worn. But at least, it looked as if someone was keeping it clean. I found his door and knocked on it.

The man who opened the door wasn't the same self-assured one I had been with an hour ago. This one looked panicked. He stepped back and let me in.

His front entry was empty other than a half-moon table beneath a mirror. His keys were tossed on top in a bowl very similar to the one I kept my keys in. Nothing out of place there.

"Come in," he said and rushed into the main room. The living room. It was well laid out. Almost elegant. Very much like its inhabitant. And it was spotless.

No evidence of a break-in.

"What am I looking for?"

"We'll start in the kitchen."

Off to the side of the living room, a galley kitchen. Updated. Clean dark cupboards and what looked to be marble countertops. Maybe he owned the apartment.

The only thing that looked out of place; six steel knives set in a row on the counter. I wandered over to them and crouched down to be eye-level with what looked to be a deliberate message. As expected, the knives looked clean of prints.

"You found them like this?"

"I sure as hell didn't do it."

"You stole my only opportunity to sleep to show me a row of knives? I thought you said this might be linked to our case."

"There's more."

Black appeared to hesitate and then walked over to a door off the living room. Must be a bedroom. I wove through his furniture and stepped through the doorway.

Whoa.

I almost took a step back. I'd never seen one before. I'd read about them. But I never thought I'd ever see one. Most of the metal rings and a suspension bar were in the vicinity of the bed.

On one wall, an assortment of bondage ropes and *toys*?

"Don't judge," Black said. "That's why I don't want forensics in here."

"Fair enough, but why bring me in?"

"I still want to follow protocol. I can't process my own crime scene."

I looked around the room. "What am I missing? I don't see a crime."

"The bedside table." Black rushed over to it and pointed at a glass sitting on its surface. So what? He forgot to do his dishes. Hardly a crime.

"This isn't my glass. I didn't leave this here."

Okay, now that *was* intriguing. "From the crime scene. The missing glass?"

"It's the same style of glass. There's even the scent of scotch in it."

I bent over the glass and sniffed it. Scotch. Black was right. Of course, he was. He could probably smell it from the next room. I looked for visible smudges from fingers.

None.

"How did they get in?"

"My balcony in the living room." He rushed past me back through the door. When I joined him, Black was squatted near an open door. "The carpet is damp. He came through here."

"How do you know it's a *he*?"

"I know the scent of my apartment. A male other than my latest guest was in here. The intruder's scent is odd. I can't get a lock on whether he's human or not."

Latest guest?

In his bedroom? With all that equipment?

Had the murder interrupted what he was doing with his *guest*?

What had he been doing in there?

A shimmer of something foreign ran up my spine.

Focus.

"How did *he* get up here?" I asked.

"I leave the door open when it's raining. Stops condensation in my windows."

"You're thirty floors up."

Black rose and walked to the open balcony door. "Can you process everything, please?"

"Do you have everything I need?"

"I keep a simple forensic kit in the front hall closet."

Of course, you do.

I retrieved the kit, slipped on some gloves, and got to work. As I moved through the apartment collecting evidence, Black stayed tethered to his sofa, sipping on an amber liquid in a glass. Every once in a while, I heard him whine. It was a very wolf-like sound. It was eerie.

This had rattled him.

Something I suspected wasn't an easy thing to do. Someone as powerful as a wolf probably didn't spook easily. I took another pass through the bedroom to make sure we hadn't missed anything. I ran my fingers over a metal ring on Black's bedpost. I wondered who would be tied to it and the other three, one on each post. Why was it the kind of release Black needed?

If he was the one being tied down, was he ever in wolf form when he was bound?

I swallowed.

None of my business.

I re-entered the living room. "All done. Just need to check the roof."

"I can do that tomorrow once I get a key from the manager." He set his glass down and rose to his feet. "You'll log everything at the station once I check out the roof?"

I held up the evidence bags I'd collected. "Once I have everything, all of it will be added to the current investigation."

"I owe you one."

"Nonsense. We're partners now."

"You won't tell anyone about my bedroom?"

"I'm not going to discuss what you do in your free time with anyone."

"Thank you."

As I waited for my taxi, I gripped the non-descript shopping bag Black had given me to carry the evidence bags. A quick shower and I would head to the station.

We had a lot of work to do.

My mind wandered back to Black's bedroom. I wasn't sure what led someone to crave bondage. There was a lot to unlock when it came to my boss. His mind was a complex place.

I crossed my arms and shivered … and not from the cold.

Black fascinated me—for more than professional reasons.

I shivered again.

Chapter Three | Mason

Seven in the morning and the bullpen was starting to fill with officers. I had been assigned four to help work the case. Four officers and Jones. I'd already argued with Sergeant Baker this morning about being assigned a babysitter. I didn't need anyone slowing me down.

Sure, Jones seemed to be intelligent, and he had come running when I called him last night—and hadn't asked questions about my bedroom.

I had decided to trust Jones.

He'd done a good job processing the scene.

Maybe it wouldn't be so bad to have him around.

I wandered over to the board that Jones had set up before I arrived at the office. He hadn't slept after being at my apartment. He'd showered, though. The scent of natural patchouli soap was strong on his skin. I stood beside him. "Any identity on our victim yet?"

"The coroner is scanning his face to see if facial recognition picks anything up."

"When will they be done?"

"Not sure. It usually takes a while."

"I recognize him."

Jones turned to me; eyebrows raised. "From where?"

"I don't know. He's not someone I've met formally, though. I caught his face in passing somewhere. Could be nothing. Might have bumped into him in the produce aisle."

"Produce aisle?" A furrow appeared between Jones' brows.

Common misconception.

"I don't just eat meat. I also eat eggs and berries. My only stop isn't the butcher."

"Oh."

There were so few of my species in the world that the majority of humans weren't well informed about us. I'm sure if I told Jones I had a functioning uterus, I might blow his mind.

It was rare to see a pregnant male Omega on the streets of Metro City. Jones probably hadn't encountered one. The environment for raising pups in the city wasn't a great one.

Like myself, most Omega males in the city were on birth control.

Whelping wolf pups could be left to places like Creekside Township.

I turned to the room. Everyone had their heads down, tapping away on keyboards. "Anyone have any information on the people staying close to our victim's suite?"

An older male human raised his hand—Maxwell. "I've just pulled the bank statements of the Dunnigans. They've been running through their savings over the past year. Could be nothing."

"Thank you." I pointed to the next hand that was up. A middle-aged female—Linda. "Yes?"

"I can confirm there were no fingerprints on the murder weapon."

"Do we even know it was the murder weapon?" Jones asked the room.

I nodded. "True. We don't know. Keep hounding forensics, Linda."

Maxwell cleared his throat. "The Dunnigans sold their house. Bought an apartment."

"Children?"

"At university."

"Could be empty nesters."

"I want to talk to them," Jones said.

"So do I." I ducked into my office and grabbed my raincoat. Maxwell handed me a slip of paper with the Dunnigan's address written on it. I handed it to Jones. He entered it in his notepad.

Not sure why Maxwell didn't just text it to us.

Old school, I guess.

Cold water from the copious patchwork of deep puddles in the station's parking lot splashed up on our shoes as Jonas and I ran for my car. We both fell into it and slammed the doors.

Jones shook his head, splattering me with droplets of rain. He wore his nondescript dirty brown hair longer than mine. Almost shaggy. I stared at the three small pinholes on his earlobe.

The fleshy lobe was dark pink from the cold dash to the car.

I looked through the windshield and started the engine. With Jones' directions, we ended up very near to my apartment block. Jones had called ahead. The Dunnigans were home.

Which concerned me. It was a Wednesday.

Why aren't they at work?

We passed by small groups of gang members, biding their time, waiting for night to fall, so they could start their drug trade in earnest. Even in broad daylight, I saw an exchange of money for drugs. They thought they were covert, laughing afterward, but they weren't. We just didn't have enough staff to put a dent in the amount of drug dealing happening throughout the city.

After we pulled up out front of our destination, I examined the building. It was an old-fashioned three-story walk-up that should have been demolished years ago to make way for a high rise. Being owned units had delayed that. It wouldn't be long until they were bought out.

Once we were buzzed up, Mitchell Dunnigan opened their apartment door. First impressions, the apartment was overly full of furniture. That spoke of a desire to either cling to a time when they owned a house, or they were hoping for an opportunity to own one again.

Jones scanned around as he sat down. Seated, he tapped away on his notepad. I suspected he had come to the same conclusion as me. Or, at least, he thought all the furniture odd.

"How can we help you?" Mitchell asked.

"We'll wait for your wife," I replied. Cathy was fussing around in the kitchen, presumably making tea. Humans always made tea when they were nervous around the police.

Sure enough, she emerged with a tea pot, four mugs, and a plate of cookies, and set them on the big coffee table in front of the seating. She held out the plate for me to partake.

I patted my stomach. "No thank you. Watching my weight." The truth was something as innocuous as a cookie would cause me untold grief. I'd be in the bathroom for days.

Jones snapped up two. I'd need to speak to him about accepting food from someone we were investigating for something like murder. I didn't detect any nefarious additions to the cookies.

He shoved one into his mouth. Little blond crumbs appeared on his lips.

I cleared my throat.

"We've been looking into your financials," I started.

Mitchell leaned forward. "Why?"

"Standard practice," Jones answered, his voice muffled behind his fisted hand. I was surprised he had cleared the cookie from his mouth so rapidly.

Maybe he didn't have a gag reflex.

Jeez, Mason.

Focus.

"We noticed you've been cleaning out your savings," I said. "Is there a reason for that?"

"That's our personal business," Mitchell snapped.

"We're just having a pleasant conversation. Tea and cookies in your home. Would you rather we arrested you both and took you down to the station?"

Cathy clung to her husband's arm. "There's no harm in telling them."

"Telling us what," Jones said.

I motioned to his notepad, indicating he needed to shut up, let me ask the questions, and just take the damned notes for the team. He lifted his finger, tipped it at me, and nodded.

Message received.

"I lost my job a year ago," Mitchell said. "Cathy has gone back to nursing, but we're having trouble making ends meet. My previous salary was significant."

"What did you do for work?"

"I was a lawyer. Criminal."

"Why did you lose your job?"

"I botched a string of high-profile cases. I was months away from making partner. They decided to bring in someone else. They didn't fire me so much as edge me out. Reduced my case load to nothing then told me I was useless to them. Gave me the opportunity to step away."

"Tell me about these cases you botched."

Mitchell sighed. "Three of them. All robberies of influential people in the city."

That's where I know his face from!

I nearly stood up. "Including the mayor, right?"

Name ... name. Rockford ... something.

I could see his face in my head. Grinning as he walked away from the courthouse, reporters crowding around him, shouting questions. Asking him how he did it—evaded conviction.

"Rockford Tennet," I blurted out.

"Who's that?" Jonas asked.

"A goddamned criminal mastermind," Mitchell said. "That's who."

"Tennet?" Jonas said. "T-E-N-N-E-T-T?"

"One T."

Tap. Tap. Tap.

"Oh, wow ... okay," Jones said, then began typing on his notepad. I assumed he was contacting the station, telling them to start a workup on our victim Rockford Tennet.

I had to admit, Jones was coming in useful. His ability to pick up what I was thinking was uncanny. I hadn't even had to tell him I recognized Rockford Tennet to be the victim.

I rose to my feet. "That's all for today. We have some information to chase up, but I want to talk to you both again. I have more questions. Please, don't leave the city."

"We had planned to visit our daughter in Riverton," Cathy said.

"Reschedule. We'll be visiting again."

I'm sure the Dunnigans were glad to see us leave. They certainly ushered us out quickly once we told them our business with them was concluded for now.

Jones and I sat in the car, the rain obscuring the view outside the windows.

"What do you think?" I asked him.

"Mitchell certainly has a motive. The victim effectively ruined his life. And a question I want to ask them next time … why were they staying in an expensive hotel when they had a perfectly good apartment in the city? If they're having money trouble, why the expense?"

"Celebration of some sort, maybe."

"Staying in the next room over certainly gave Mitchell opportunity."

"I think if Mitchell had done it, his wife would have been more rattled by us being there today. She was nervous but she wasn't giving off terror-level pheromones."

Jones blinked at me, watching me as if trying to figure me out. He'd obviously never worked with a wolf before. My heightened senses were throwing him off.

"Seems a bit of a coincidence, though," Jones said. "Being in the next room to a guy whom he fought against in court. A guy who wiped out his career. I don't like coincidences."

"No. Neither do I. Put together a new set of questions for Mitchell. We can visit them again tonight once we find out more about the victim."

We arrived back in the bullpen to a flurry of activity. The board had a picture of Rockford Tennet at its center. Around the picture were sticky notes with the start of details of his life.

"What do we know about Rockford?" I asked the room.

Maxwell stood. "Rockford Tennet. Thirty-four. Alpha wolf from the Stony Creek pack up north. Career criminal. Spend some time in prison for theft and assault. He's been released without charge more times than he's been convicted. Smooth operator."

"And his personal life?" I prompted.

"Now, that is interesting," Linda said. "Rockford has a twin brother, Benedict Tennet. Eight years ago, they lost both their parents in a car accident."

I looked at the board to see if someone else had caught an important piece of information. My team had missed it completely. "The owners of Tennet Technologies."

Linda stared at her notes. The scent of her perspiration reached my senses. She was embarrassed. "Yes, that would track. Rockford stood to inherit a large amount of money."

"How much are we talking?" Jones asked.

"Multiples of millions."

"Why do you say *stood* to inherit?" I asked.

"His parents had written him out of the will. They left everything to Benedict."

"That couldn't have gone over well."

Jones handed me his electronic notepad. On its screen a story about one of the robberies Mitchell Dunnigan had tried in court. Rockford had been accused of breaking into his childhood home where his brother lived, cracking the safe, and stealing jewelry and a large amount of cash.

The case had fallen apart due to lack of physical proof, even though Rockford had taunted Benedict, telling him he'd come into some money out of nowhere—and laughed about it.

"I want to know more about this brother," I said to Jones.

"I'll get on it. Work up a profile for him, but I need to grab a cup of coffee first."

"Hurry." I put my hand on Jones' substantial shoulder and gave him a little shove. It was a habit I had never succumbed to. Coffee. I couldn't understand the appeal of it. It tasted bitter. Plus, I wasn't sure what the shot of caffeine would do to my already amped-up system.

Jones reappeared, coffee in hand, and slipped behind his desk.

I had to bite my lip to keep from laughing. I wandered over to his desk.

"Nice cup," I said as I got a better look at it. "Your cats?" The cup had a photo of two cats. One black. The other a tabby. They were seated in front of a Christmas tree, wearing festive hats.

Jones' ears turned the color of ripe apples. "It was a gift."

My partner was more nervous than he should be. His scent had changed, now laced with something bordering on excitement. His entire essence filled my senses. The pheromones being released by his body were similar to those secreted when a human was sexually aroused.

It made my cock stir.

He *wanted* me to uncover the true origins of the cup.

Not sure why.

"From whom?" I asked. "You? Was it a Christmas gift to yourself?"

"Guilty." Jones looked up at me, a shy smile on his face. The pure innocence of it and the gift he had given himself made my heart stutter a little. He gave off a very boy-next-door vibe.

I cleared my throat. "Get to work. I want to know everything about the brother." I turned to Maxwell. "Send me everything you have on Rockford's criminal record."

"Yes, sir."

That word gave me a little thrill. *Sir.* As a wolf, I never thought I would one day make detective and have humans working for me. And be called *sir*.

Not only that, but the department had given me my own office. I didn't have a desk in the open office like many other junior detectives. The theory I had risen in the ranks and been given perks because I was a minority—and a wolf as well … had a lot of weight to it.

With this case, though, I was going to earn this office.

Linda burst to her feet. "We have the report back from forensics."

Finally.

"What did they find?"

"A whole lot of nothing. The soil on the carpet came from the landscaping below the suite. And it was the same as the soil on the roof."

"And the suite? Any evidence?"

"DNA from the victim but no decipherable prints on anything. The room was miraculously clean for a hotel room. Their cleaning staff must be well trained."

"Tell me about the glasses."

"The one in the suite had residue of Rohypnol in it. The one in your apartment—nothing nefarious other than scotch. Both had DNA from Rockford."

"Send me the coroner's reports, please."

I retreated to my office.

I left my office door open. I'd rather have it closed, but I understood leaving it open made me seem more approachable, and that the misconception would be beneficial to the case.

I brought my computer to life, opened the file Maxwell had sent me, and started scanning through the information. Maxwell was right. Rockford had been arrested quite a few times, mainly because of his association with other criminals who had links to the crimes. I scrolled through his detention interviews. Over the past fifteen years, he was often a person of interest.

The only time he'd been incarcerated was when he'd been caught *holding the bag*. Jewelry and cash from an affluent family's vault. Even though there was no evidence of him inside the house. The case that had lost Mitchell Dunnigan his job—the robbery of the mayor. An alleged accomplice of

Rockford's had turned on him, telling the police Rockford was the architect of the scheme he'd been picked up for. That Rockford's job had been to crack the safe.

Safes that can be cracked easier if you're not wearing gloves.

No fingerprints.

Our victim had no fingerprints.

Even with the accusation, a lack of an alibi, and traffic cameras placing Rockford in the area, there was no evidence our victim was ever in the house he was accused of robbing.

In addition to no fingerprints, the guy was a ghost.

He knew how to cover his tracks.

So, who wanted him dead?

A knock on my doorframe broke my thoughts.

"So, his brother," Jones started. "No love lost there. Rockford sued his brother for a share of the inheritance. He was unsuccessful. The night following the verdict, Rockford broke into the family home where Benedict lives and attacked him. A housekeeper called the police."

"Was he charged?"

"Slap on the wrist. Five-thousand dollar fine for assault."

I scrolled down through the information on my screen. There it was. The assault charge. And it wasn't Rockford's first one. He had assault charges toward his domestic partner as well.

I read the details of the abuse reports.

Jeezus.

The similarities were stunning.

I clenched my fist and clamped down on my mouse, the description of the domestic assaults making my gut churn. What did you expect? He'd been assaulted by his partner. Two wolves. There had been significant injuries. It took every molecule of my being not to start trembling.

Calm down.

It's done and over with. You never have to see him again.

"Black? You all right?"

"Find out more about his ex-domestic partner. His chosen mate."

I wasn't sure if Jones would understand the distinction between chosen and fated. Rockford's mate had no obligation to stay with him. They weren't fated mates, but he'd chosen to endure years of abuse at Rockford's hands. He'd stuck around and just taken it—day in and day out.

My neck prickled with heat.

Jones vacated the doorway to my office. I couldn't contain my emotional state. Late at night, I still woke up— terrified he was back. I launched myself at my door and slammed it shut.

I didn't make it back across the room to my desk. I slid down the door, my back against it, landed on my ass, and wrapped my arms around my head as I placed my forehead on my knees.

And broke open.

Part panic—part despair.

I knew it was best to let the tears flow. They cleared my system. Once they were gone, I could re-ground myself. Put the wolf who had controlled me for so many years back in his locked box. I waited until my breathing evened out before opening my door and returning to my desk. I guarded against any more interruptions from my memory. I could revisit them at home.

Maybe have a *guest* over.

Work through some emotional pain by way of physical discomfort.

Jones poked his head in the door. "I have an address for the ex-partner, Bryan. He's working from home today. He's a bit hesitant but he says he'll talk to us." He frowned. "Considering the level of domestic violence, Bryan was agonizingly upset when I told him Rockford was dead."

"Bryan probably loved him. Maybe still does."

Too close to home.

Jones shook his head. "Doesn't mean he's not the killer."

"No, that's true." I joined Jones at the door. "Let's go."

Jones rattled out information as I drove. The history between Rockford and his ex-partner. How they had grown up together. How they had been on the varsity football team. When he was done with that, he switched to his suspicion of the concierge. How he had acted strangely.

Then came stories of his own life playing football in high school. How his first girlfriend had been a cheerleader. How when he'd gone away to university, he'd lost her.

Then about how his mom had suffered while he was away for four years, not able to take care of herself. And how agonizing the decision to go away to school had been for him.

Then how his mom had died of an overdose two years ago.

Then back to the case.

I relaxed my shoulders.

Jones' voice calmed me.

Before we went to visit Rockford's ex-partner, we needed to break the news to Rockford's brother about his death. One of my officers had texted Jones with the address of Benedict's office. He had taken over as president of Tennet Technologies when his parents passed away.

We circled the office building a few times until I finally decided to descend into the underground parking. Both Jones and I placed our hands on our department-issue revolvers as we made our way to the elevator. Predictably, the area around it smelled like urine. Even in a fancy building like this, it couldn't be avoided. The door opened, revealing the presence of an attendant sitting on a stool in the corner. It was customary for the attendant to push the button for your desired floor for you. This one was too busy on his phone, typing at a furious pace.

Jones reached past him and pressed *sixteen*. The top floor. Not an incredibly tall building but Tennet Technologies occupied every floor of the high-rise. They were worth billions.

Not only had Rockford missed out on an inheritance, but it also seemed he had nothing to do with the running of the family business either. What had the falling out been about?

I approached the receptionist directly in front of the elevator as it opened. It appeared this might be a private, complete-floor office. I only detected five humans on the entire level.

I flashed my identification and badge. "We need to see Mr. Tennet."

"He's in a meeting."

I waggled the badge at her. "Tell him his meeting is over."

She pinched her eyebrows at me and then picked up the phone. "I'm sorry, Mr. Tennet, but there's a Detective Black here to see you." She chewed on her bottom lip. "He didn't say."

"It's about his brother," I said to clarify.

"It's about your brother."

The receptionist pulled the phone away from her ear as a long string of colorful curse words carried through the phone line. Then I heard what sounded like a mumbled apology.

"He'll see you now."

I pointed at a door, and she nodded. Through the door, a short hallway, and a set of double doors. I tapped on the door and let myself in, Jones close behind me. Inside was an immense office. Wood paneling stretched from the doorway almost 20 feet to a set of floor-to-ceiling windows. In front of those windows, an imposing wolf.

The identical facial features were uncanny.

Rockford and Benedict were true twins.

He lifted a glass of scotch to his lips, sipped, then set the glass on his desk.

I focused on the glass. It might be a coincidence but the glass on Benedict's desk was an exact match to the ones we had found in the hotel room and my apartment.

And he was drinking scotch.

I checked over my shoulder.

Jones was staring at the glass, his brow furrowed. He had noticed it too.

"What has my brother done this time?"

I crossed the room to him. "I'm afraid I have bad news."

"He's killed someone. I knew he would eventually."

"Why do you say that?" Jones asked.

"My brother is a vicious son of a bitch. Can't control his temper."

"As of late last night, he won't be killing anyone," I said.

Benedict dropped into the chair behind his desk. "He's dead?"

"I'm sorry."

He waved his hand at me. "Don't be. It was bound to happen someday. My brother didn't exactly live a safe, law-abiding life." He leaned forward. "How did he die?"

"We can't give you details ... but he *was* murdered."

"Dammit, Rockford. You stupid idiot."

"Do you have any idea why he might have been staying at the Grand Metro?"

"Is that where he died?"

"It is."

Benedict played with his glass, spinning it on the desk. "Room 1410?"

Jones stepped closer to the desk.

"How did you know that?" I asked.

"We keep that room for when people associated with the business stay in the city."

"Would anyone have known he was there?"

"My receptionist would have received a call, saying the room had been occupied by him."

"And she would tell you?"

"Sometimes ... but she didn't this time."

"And he would be allowed to do that? Occupy the room?"

Benedict slumped back in his chair. "My brother didn't always have accommodation. I'm not a complete monster. I didn't want him in my house, but I didn't want him on the street either."

"This suite, 1410, how long have you had an ongoing reservation on it?"

Benedict jutted his bottom lip out in thought. "I don't know. Six years."

"Enough time for any number of people to know about it."

"Yeah, I guess."

"Why didn't your brother have money for accommodations?" This was a curiosity. If Rockford had completed the heists he'd been accused of, he shouldn't have had money problems.

"He's ... *was* an addict."

"Drugs?"

"Gambling. Came to me about a month ago, begging for me to help him. He owed some money he'd lost during poker games. He was desperate. Some shady people were after him."

"Did you help him?"

"Told him he needed to seek professional guidance. A twelve-step program—something."

"But you didn't give him money?"

Benedict finished the scotch in his glass. "Wish I had. Do you think that's who killed him?"

"We're still making initial inquiries. Early days."

"So, you and your brother didn't get along," Jones said.

I relaxed my shoulders. Jones asked intelligent questions. There was no reason I should stop him other than my own ego. We were partners. I decided to let him be one.

"We were inseparable when we were kids. The whole twin thing. We did everything together. It wasn't until high school that things changed. He met that Bryan on his football team."

"His ex-partner?"

Benedict sighed. "Yeah. Wow, he was obsessed with that wolf. When Bryan agreed to start seeing Rockford, my brother went from obsessed to paranoid. From day one, he believed Bryan was cheating on him. Tried to drag me along to stalk his movements. Of course, I refused."

That was something we could get into more when we talked to Bryan.

I had a more pressing question.

"Why was your brother written out of your parents' will?" I asked.

"I don't honestly know. He did something that upset Mother—in the extreme. She refused to see Rockford. We couldn't even say his name. Wish I knew what it was."

"And when he sued you?"

"The courts refused to budge on the will. Ruled in my favor."

"You could have given him the money he thought he was owed."

"I offered to set up a trust for him. Told him if he cleaned up his act and came to work for the business, I would release the money to him in monthly amounts."

"He didn't like that," Jones said.

"He assaulted me. Called me controlling."

"He received a five thousand dollar fine," I said.

"And *I* paid it."

"You did? Weren't you the one who pressed charges?"

"I was hoping they'd put him in prison. Give him some time to cool off. Maybe think more clearly about my offer. I was hoping to get my brother back."

"And he was qualified to work in the business?" Jones asked.

"Rockford had a master's in business. Plus, it's in his blood. He was more than qualified."

"What happened? Why did he turn to crime instead?" I asked.

Benedict threw up his hands. "If only I knew."

"Tell me about when you thought he broke in."

Benedict swished one hand through the air. "There was no evidence. He rubbed my face in it; the fact he had pulled off a heist the police had little chance in hell of solving."

"You knew he was talking about the items you'd had stolen."

"Listed them in detail."

"That must have made you mad," Jones said.

"Not mad enough to kill him. I loved my brother."

"Okay, thank you, Mr. Tennet," I said, closing the interview. "That's it for now."

Benedict rose from his desk. "When can I have my brother's body?"

"It'll be a while yet. It's a murder investigation. He's viewed as evidence."

"Can I see him, at least?"

"We can arrange that. I'll have the coroner call you." I reached forward and shook Benedict's hand. "And again, we're sorry for your loss."

Back in the car, Jones clung to his notepad, scrolling through what looked to be a report. He tapped the screen and turned to face me. "It's confirmed. The utility knife is the murder weapon."

"What else does the report say?"

"No foreign DNA on the body but he was dosed to the hilt with a sedative."

"And DNA on the utility knife?"

"Contaminated by those pigeons."

I had questions buzzing around in my head.

"How much do you think Rockford weighed?"

"I can tell you exactly what he weighs." He flicked through pages of the coroner's report until he reached the front page. "6 foot 7. 270 pounds."

Yeah, he was big.

I thought back to Mitchell sitting on a recliner in his living room. Soaking wet, the human probably only weighed 200 pounds. And he was middle-aged. Hauling a body the size of Rockford's for any distance would be nearly impossible for someone of his stature and age.

And why would Mitchell have reported the ice machine if he was the one using it?

"Check one final thing for me to do with the Dunnigans." I started the car. "Have someone contact the climbing businesses in the city. See if Mitchell—or Benedict have taken any classes in the last couple of years. Or rented any equipment recently."

"On it." Jones started typing. "Although, someone like Benedict would have hired someone to kill his brother. I highly doubt he would have done it himself."

"You're right and that complicates things."

"Are we headed to Bryan's now?"

I liked how eager Jones was, but he was a human and humans needed regular sustenance. He probably hadn't even eaten breakfast. "When was the last time you ate?"

"Um." Jones looked at me, his eyelashes batting open and closed. They accentuated his soulful brown eyes. My gaze wandered from his eyes to his lips and back again.

He had a kind face.

"Yesterday sometime," he replied.

I cranked the wheel, headed for a bodega I knew of in the area. I wasn't an expert on where to find human food in the city, but I sometimes stopped for cubes of steak at this one.

I pulled up outside. "Get something to eat."

Jones peered at me, not moving to open his door. He looked suspicious. "Why?"

"Because you need to eat."

His gaze focused on my eyes as if they would tell him something. "And you'll be here when I get back? You're not going to take off on me, right?"

"What makes you think I'd do that?"

I smirked at him.

"You don't have a good track record."

"It's a bad area. I'm not going to leave you here."

"Promise?"

"Jones … I trusted you with my secret. You can trust me with something as simple as not abandoning you at a bodega." I shoved his shoulder. "Go. Just skip anything with garlic. I can't stand the smell of the stuff. Bring any into my car and I will have to ditch your ass."

Jones was reluctant but hunger won out, and he jogged into the store. The car was far too quiet without him sharing the space with me. I was waiting for it. I knew he was dying to tell me about his cats. Just to fuck with him, I pulled the car down half a block.

Chapter Four | Arnie

I came to an abrupt stop as I exited the bodega with a pastrami, lettuce, and Swiss cheese sandwich in hand. Of course, the car was gone. What had I expected?

I looked up and down the street. Half a block away, I spotted Black's ugly green car.

Asshole.

I couldn't contain the grin, though. I must be growing on him if he hadn't abandoned me completely and had a squad car pick me up. I knew I had broken my new rule of slowing down on the talking, but Black hadn't stopped me, and he seemed like the kind of guy who would.

Wolf.

The kind of *wolf* who would.

It was going to take some getting used to. Working alongside a guy whose body could shift from human form to the body of a wolf. It defied biology and physics, yet there it was—a creature unlike any other in the entire world. Wolf shifters were unique in their physiology.

I slid into the passenger seat and bit into my sandwich.

"Lettuce?" Black said. "Not sure how you humans can eat that stuff. Did you know it makes you smell funny? Like a summer afternoon at the dump."

I wrinkled my nose at the thought. Maybe I'd skip the lettuce next time.

"What does Bryan do for work?" Black asked.

"Stockbroker."

"Does he have a new partner? A mate?"

I set my sandwich on the dash and opened my notes. "He does. A Justin Samson. A few years younger than him. They've been together for over five years as far as we can tell. That's how long they've been filing taxes together as a couple."

"Grab your sandwich." Black waited for me to lift it, then eased the car into traffic. It seemed stockbrokers did well for themselves. An hour from the city, we arrived outside a *house*.

An oddity in accommodation.

"Money isn't a problem," I said.

"Doesn't look like it."

After we knocked, the front door of the house was opened by a beautiful and delicate-looking man. I didn't usually consider men to be beautiful, but this guy was stunning.

Even more stunning than Black.

"Can I help you?"

"We're here to see Bryan," Black answered. "He's expecting us."

"Oh, the police." He stepped back to let us in. "Come in. I'll get Bryan for you." He pointed toward the living room through a set of columns off the front entry.

Black and I made ourselves comfortable on the sofa.

We were soon joined by a handsome, somewhat larger-than-me, man.

Wolf.

We were dealing with wolves in this case.

I wondered if Bryan's partner Justin was one. He certainly didn't have the stature of a wolf.

Bryan dropped into a chair across from us. His face looked drawn, tired, and blotchy, and his eyes were rimmed with dark pink as if he'd been crying.

"I'm sorry," Black started.

"I can't believe he's gone," Bryan said. He clenched his hands together as if trying to control his emotions. Either he was a good actor, or he hadn't known Rockford was dead before we told him. When I'd spoken to him on the phone, he'd become inconsolable.

His partner, Justin, had come on the line and excused Bryan from continuing the call.

"We need to ask you some questions," Black said.

"I'll tell you what I can."

"How long had you known Rockford?"

"Since high school. We were on the football team together. My family had just moved into Metro City. Rockford started flirting with me—day one. I'd never imagined myself with a male before I met him. He was charming and respectful, not pushing me to go out with him."

"But you finally did," I said.

Bryan laughed softly. "He finally wore me down. And for the first month, he was sweet and attentive. Then he changed. He started asking about my friends. Wanted to meet all of them. Which wasn't weird in itself. We were going out together. But he was so adamant about it. Then after he met them, he said he didn't like them. Started taking me out practically every night. I just thought he wanted to be with me all the time. That he really liked me."

"He was trying to separate you from them," Black said.

Bryan nodded. "Exactly. Looking back, I can see that. At the time, I was too young to understand controlling personality red flags. I thought he just liked me a lot."

"When did the abuse start?" Black asked.

"Not for about two years. First year in college. We were living in the dorms. Not together but on the same floor. He had a habit of *not* knocking before he entered my dorm room as if he was trying to catch me and my roommate up to something.

Before the start of college, he had told me he loved me and wanted to spend forever with me. I mistook jealousy for love."

Bryan hung his head and looked at the floor. "The first time he hit me, it shocked me to my core. It was just a slap across the face. But I felt like I deserved it."

"Why?" I asked.

"We were supposed to meet for dinner. I lost track of time, having a few beers with some new friends I met on campus. Rockford sat in the restaurant for over an hour waiting for me."

"What happened after he hit you?" Black asked, except his voice was quiet and low like he didn't want to know the answer. I checked on him. He had his arms wrapped around his stomach.

"He immediately apologized profusely. Kept stroking my face and kissing me. Begging me to never do that to him again. That he'd been so scared and worried about me."

"And the next time?" I asked.

Bryan's shoulders slumped. "It just got worse from there, but I loved him. It wasn't until he started attacking me in wolf form and I ended up in the hospital that I gave my head a shake."

Justin wandered into the room, sat on the arm of Bryan's chair, put his arm around Bryan's shoulder, and kissed his head. It was then that I noticed Justin's hands. They were misshapen; his fingers extremely long and lean, bony, each one of his tendons on the top of his hand protruding.

He squeezed Bryan around the shoulders, then left the room.

My face must have made it apparent I had questions.

"He has a rare bone condition," Bryan said. "His entire frame looks like that."

Bryan was a sizeable wolf. I couldn't imagine Justin and him being intimate. Anyone that fragile looking had to be breakable. The look they'd exchanged—they were deeply in love.

Black looked perturbed, his brows drawn, noticeably inhaling.

My partner was distracted.

"Does your mate keep birds?" Black asked.

"Yeah, pigeons. Why?"

Black shook his head. "Not sure how you can stand the smell."

"You started pressing charges against Rockford," I said, getting the interview back on track.

"I thought it would stop him from hurting me. Bring back the wolf who had been so attentive and sweet to me in high school."

"Why didn't you fight back?" I asked. "You're a big wolf."

"I considered standing up for myself, using my size, but I loved him so much … I didn't want to hurt him."

I shook my head. I had no experience with domestic abuse. I would never even pretend to understand the motivation behind staying with an abuser.

Black surged to his feet. "All right. Thank you."

I hadn't realized we were finished.

I had to be quick to catch up to Black as he saw himself out. Not even a *stay in the city* was uttered to Bryan. He started the car before I had even closed my door.

Something was up.

I reached for his arm to get his attention.

He flinched and pulled his arm away.

Okay. No touching.

"What was going on in there?" I asked.

"Domestic violence cases bother me."

"They bother everyone. Your reaction in there was visceral." There was only one reason I could think of for Black's reaction. He had personal experience with that kind of abuse.

I decided to drop it. "Where to next?" I asked.

"I'd like to speak to the concierge."

"Are we going to take a chance that he's working?"

"Yeah, I'd like to catch him off guard. You said he was jumpy. Maybe he knows something in addition to being touchy about us going on the roof."

My phone dinged.

Maxwell.

"Benedict was in the military for many years. Maybe he learned how to repel and ascend as part of his training."

"That's very likely," Black said, "but I'm having trouble establishing motive with him. If he loved his brother and wanted to help him reform, why would he kill him?"

"What about the people Rockford owed money to?"

Black sighed. "Finding out who he might have owed money to would take a level of resources I don't have access to. I'd need to put officers undercover. Not going to happen."

What?

"So, we might be hobbled from solving this case? That's bullshit."

"That's called bureaucracy. I have a budget I have to follow."

Fuck.

I crossed my arms, shoved my back against the seat, and slumped down. My first murder case, and we might not be able to solve it because of financial issues. Goddamned red tape.

"That doesn't upset you?" I asked.

"Of course, it does." Black patted my thigh. "Let's run through our suspects again."

Miraculously, Black's touch pulled me out of my funk. I longed for him to put his hand back on my thigh. The realization that I desired his physical attention shook me.

And made me blush.

My ears burned.

And Black noticed. He stared at me; his lips parted.

I swallowed and broke eye contact with him. "Suspects."

"Yes, let's start with Mitchell. He had motive *and* opportunity. Rockford was instrumental in him losing his well-paying job. And he was in the suite next door to the murder."

"Means is a bit shaky. How did he get from his suite to Rockford's? Plus, Rockford was a big guy. Mitchell would have needed to place him in the tub. No small feat given Mitchell's size."

"What about Benedict?" Black asked.

"Not sure of his motive. Maybe he hated his brother; his talk of loving him and trying to help might be a story he wove for us. We have no way of fact-checking him on those things."

"He had the opportunity. His receptionist might have told him that Rockford was staying in the room. He saw his opportunity and used his military training to get into it."

"And Bryan?" I asked. I suspected I knew the answer.

"He didn't do it."

"How can you be so sure?"

"It takes a deep level of love to put up with that much abuse. He'll never be free of it. It'll haunt him for the rest of his life. He'll have even considered going back to him."

I exhaled.

Jeezus.

My partner was hanging onto some heavy pain. I wasn't going to push him about Bryan. For now, I was going to trust Black's instinct.

"You were doing some heavy inhaling in Bryan's house. What was with that?"

"Damned birds."

"That's it?"

Black backed out of Bryan's driveway and pulled onto the road. "No, his partner, Justin's scent. It's practically non-existent. Threw me off. Only detected a faint scent of granola bars."

"I eat a lot of those."

"I know."

It was going to take me a while to get used to that; the fact Black was so aware of my scent. It made me feel exposed. I wondered if he could detect my growing attraction to him.

We pulled up outside the Grand Metro. Black used the valet to have the car parked for us. Luckily, the concierge I had encountered last night was back at the desk. I looked at my phone. We'd spent a lot of time weaving through traffic today. It was almost 6 pm.

I'd known Black for less than 24 hours.

Then why?

My body was feeling some intense things for him.

"Can I help you?" the concierge asked.

"Yes, you can take a break and talk to us," Black replied as he showed his badge.

"I'll get my manager to cover the desk. Just a moment."

The desk now occupied by an older man in an expensive suit, the concierge led us to a conference room down a broad hallway. He flicked on the lights and took a seat across the table from us. His suit hugged and strained atop his broad shoulders and thick arms.

The man could double as the hotel's bouncer if they had one.

He would have had no trouble arranging an incapacitated Rockford in the tub.

"Your full name," Black asked.

"Daniel Richardson." He shifted in his seat, obviously uncomfortable being with us. I looked at his suit. I had a concern. His clothes would have been wet after being on the outside of the building. Would he have had enough time to change his clothes before I saw him at the desk?

"Do you make a habit of keeping extra suits in your locker?" Black asked.

I smiled. Less than a day and we were syncing up already.

"Not typically, no."

"When would be a non-typical example?" I asked.

"If I was going to work a double shift … I might want to change."

Why?

I wore the same suit for days. Nothing to do with the fact I only had two. I couldn't afford the dry cleaning. I was still paying off my student loans.

"Or I'm helping with a banquet," Daniel continued. "My clothes might get dirty."

"Why didn't you want us on the roof?" Black asked.

"Because it's not safe up there. A lot of those capstones are loose."

"You spend a lot of time up there?" I asked.

Daniel looked toward the door. I checked over my shoulder. No one was there.

"I go up there to smoke."

"Cigarettes?"

"Marijuana."

"Another reason you might want to change your clothes," Black said.

Daniel nodded.

"Do you know about room 1410?" I asked.

"Only that it's held by Tennet Technologies for their guests."

"Did you know someone was staying in that room last night?"

"Yes, I checked him in."

"His name wasn't in the computer."

Daniel hung his head. "Rockford likes his privacy."

"First name basis?" Black said.

"We went to high school together."

Wow. okay.

"Did you know *Bryan*?" I asked.

"Rockford's high school boyfriend? Sure, we all knew about their relationship."

"Were you friends with them?"

"No, but for a few weeks, I tutored Bryan in Physics. Until Rockford showed up at my house, accused me of sleeping with his boyfriend, and threatened to *end me*." Air quotes.

"Nothing was happening between you and Bryan?" Black asked.

"I'm not gay."

Boyfriend. Gay. I knew enough to know those weren't words wolves used. Daniel was obviously human. "Did you and Rockford ever smooth things over?"

Daniel shook his head. "He continued to breathe down my neck for the rest of high school. He was convinced I was seeing Bryan behind his back."

"What of your current interactions with Rockford," Black said. "Were they civil?"

Daniel's jaw jerked to one side and his eyes became hooded beneath his eyebrows. A guy who had seemed harmless a moment ago suddenly turned dangerous looking.

"That bastard threatened to have me fired. Told me he'd tell my boss I stole money from his room. Bragged that he could put the money in my work locker because of his lack of prints."

"You knew about that—his lack of fingerprints?" I asked.

"He told everyone. He and his twin brother both. No fingerprints."

I almost rolled my eyes. We'd forgotten to ask Benedict about his fingerprints. Tiredness was catching up with both of us. After this interview, we needed to call it a night.

"What was stopping him from doing that? Following through?" Black asked.

Daniel's face flushed crimson and he looked down at his hands.

"It's impossible to find a good job in this city. Having a theft on my employment record would have ruined me. I would have ended up homeless."

I leaned forward. "What did you have to do?"

Daniel didn't speak right away. Then his voice came out in a whisper. "When he stayed in the hotel … I would have to *visit* him in his room."

"Sex," Black guessed.

"Just blow jobs."

"Were you in his room last night?" I asked.

"For a few minutes. He orgasmed, we argued about our arrangement—and I left."

"What time was that?"

Daniel looked up. "Around 8:30. During my break."

"Have you ever done any recreational climbing?" Black asked.

"Just in Boy Scouts."

"All right," Black said, standing. "Thank you for your time. Please don't leave town."

"I didn't think I had a choice with Rockford," Daniel said. "I didn't want to lose my job."

"We're not judging you," I assured him. "Work is scarce."

Inside, I disagreed with Daniel. I would never perform sexual favors to keep my job. But then, I had a university degree. That afforded me a measure of protection from destitution.

Privilege.

I checked myself.

In Daniel's world, he'd believed he didn't have a choice.

Back in the car, surrounded by the scent of Black's cologne, I nodded off. When I awoke, we were outside my apartment building. The usual suspects were lurking outside the door.

"I want to meet your cats," Black blurted out as I placed my hand on the door handle.

My eyebrows jerked up as I looked across the dark car, searching his faint features to determine if he was messing with me. The bizarre request had come out of nowhere. I hadn't even talked about my cats today other than the brief exchange we'd had because of my mug.

"You do?"

"I like cats."

"To eat?"

Black snorted and laughed. "No, some of the pack mates I grew up with had cats. Their Uncle Patrick rescued two kittens for them. Their sire wasn't impressed, but he let them keep them. I haven't been around any cats since then. I have a bit of nostalgia for them."

"Their sire?"

"Father."

"Oh." I considered. "Okay, if you promise not to eat them, you can come in." I hauled myself out of the car and led Black to the door of my building.

The crowd of men blocked our way. I was going to say something to get them to move, but over my right shoulder came a sound that chilled me through. A growl the depth and viciousness of which I had never heard from a dog.

It gave me goosebumps.

And a little thrill as the men scurried away from the door. I was very conscious of Black's presence behind me as I took the stairs up to my floor. Not the steady sound of his boots as they hit the steps, but a sense of security, knowing he was there watching my back.

He wasn't even breathing heavily when we completed the ten sets of stairs. It took me all of two seconds to see that my apartment door was broken open.

I raced down the exterior hallway and burst through the splintered pieces.

I didn't care about my safety. My only thought—are my cats all right?

Black jumped through the door behind me and shoved what he could of it closed. Again, I sensed him at my back. Knew he would be right behind me.

I tore around the apartment, calling for them, searching under the sofa, chairs, and the bed. Not finding them, I raced past Black and onto the exterior hallway.

They were nowhere to be seen.

"You're looking for your cats." Black's voice was right in my ear.

"They're not in the apartment."

"I can smell them out here." He stepped around me and pointed to the left. "They took off down that way. Is there any way for them to get out of the building?"

"They could take the stairs to the first floor and leap onto the main concourse down there." I looked over the edge of the waist-high wall, searching the darkness for them. My heart was thundering. I closed my eyes as Black placed his hand on my shoulder.

"Come back into the apartment," he said.

"But you said they're out here."

"Trust me." Black gripped my elbow and guided me back inside. His touch was gentle and confident and sent fingers of crackling sizzles up my skin. My breath caught in my chest.

I'd never trusted someone as much.

"I'll find them," he said.

Before I could ask how, he started stripping off his clothes, and laying them on the back of a chair. I had to turn away when he hooked his thumbs into the waistband of his tight black briefs. The parts of his naked body I had seen had left me feeling weak.

I almost forgot about my cats.

I could picture him in my mind now.

I nearly groaned.

That image of him nearly nude was going to haunt me.

The guttural grunting noises behind me made me spin back around. A creature—half man—half wolf was at my feet, his flesh looking like it was boiling. I jumped back as a bone thrust up and jammed against his skin, and he whined. He was on all fours, barely able to stand.

Crack—snap.

Jerk—twist.

Again and again, until I felt like I was going to throw up.

I covered my ears.

It was the most brutal thing I'd ever encountered.

What had been lightly covered in fur became a thick pelt of grey, his pale ivory skin disappearing beneath it. It was his changing face that was most disturbing. His stunning features, his green eyes, full lashes, high cheekbones, and full pink lips—disappeared, stretching all out of shape until I thought for sure, his skin was going to tear. Most of his body resembling a wolf, he collapsed on the ground, panting. The last of his fur filled in as his face finished forming.

He'd just gone through an incredible amount of pain—for my cats.

He leaped to his feet, sniffing, and snarling low in his throat. I stepped back. I wasn't sure how much of *detective* Black was still in there. He must have sensed my discomfort.

He whined and touched my dangling fingers with his cold nose, then took off past my broken door. He was taking an incredible risk for me. I knew shifting was banned in the city.

I sank onto my ass on the floor and waited.

The sounds of cats shrieking and fighting something off had me springing to my feet, frantic, running onto the exterior hallway, and looking into the courtyard below, scanning.

Nothing.

Agonizing moments passed after they fell quiet.

What if he killed them?

To my left—the sound of an angry cat. My pulse thrummed in my ears. The sight of a grey wolf jogging toward me with one of my cats in its mouth not terrifying me in the least.

He dropped Mittens at my feet and took off back to where he had come from. Presumably down to the courtyard to collect Carlos. I lifted the black cat into my arms.

She was wet from Black's saliva, but she was unharmed.

My family was complete when Black set my orange tabby at my feet. I held them both under my nose and kissed their little heads. They smelled heavily of dog.

Black stepped back when I coughed and sneezed.

It seemed I was allergic to *wolf* Black.

With my nose running and my eyes stinging, I whispered a heartfelt, "Thank you," to him. I wasn't sure if he understood me or not. I believed he did. His current state fascinated me.

I wanted to know more.

I hoped he would tell me more.

He looked toward my door and whined. I knew what he wanted. I carried the cats into my apartment ahead of him, then left Black alone in the living room to shift and dress in privacy.

I locked the cats in my bedroom after giving them some loving.

The sound of my door being forced into place filled the front entry as I made my way to the living room. Black somehow managed to close and partially latch the door.

It had taken an incredible amount of strength to rearrange the pieces of wood.

Black hadn't donned his suit jacket, and he wasn't wearing his tie. His buttons were open enough to show off his chest, and he'd rolled up his sleeves, exposing his muscular forearms.

I reached for the wall for support.

Jeezus.

He was beautiful.

"It doesn't lock, but at least the cats can't get out," Black said, dusting off his hands. He looked up and smiled at me. The smile reached his eyes. It was the first time I'd seen him look happy. Not a smart-ass smirk. Not a laughing after ditching me smile.

Happy.

My heart thudded in my chest.

Fuck, you're in trouble.

I found my voice. "You have no idea how thankful I am, Black."

"Mason."

Mason? First names? I wasn't sure how to process the spontaneous shift in our relationship. It was true, I'd seen his bedroom-slash-playroom, and he'd saved my cats by shifting into a wolf.

We *had* stepped away from a conventional partner relationship.

"Arnie."

Mason laughed and covered his mouth, creating crinkle lines near his eyes.

"Your name is Arnold?"

"Ha. Ha." I smiled at him. "Some of us don't have cool names like Mason."

Mason stopped laughing and lowered his hand from his mouth. "I'm sorry. It just caught me off guard. Don't hear of many Arnolds. I like that your name is *Arnie*. It suits you."

"Why?"

"Makes you sound sophisticated."

"But I'm not."

"Maybe you are." Mason's throat visibly bobbed; he seemed nervous.

I licked my lips as my gaze wandered all over him. I didn't mean to be so obvious. I couldn't stop myself. His eyes were fixed on me. When he took a step toward me, I took a step back.

"Do you think my break-in is linked to the case?" I asked, interrupting the seriously insane tension between us. I surveyed the room. The television and my laptop were missing.

"I smell the guys from outside in here," Mason said.

"So, you think it was them?"

"Anything else missing besides the television?"

"My laptop. I don't have much. Nothing was disturbed in the bedroom."

"I think it's safe to say your intruders have no link to our case."

I crossed my arms. "I hate that I know who it is … but I can't do anything about it."

"You're afraid of retribution."

"I'm lucky they leave me alone as much as they do. I turned my back on the gang."

"And they just let you go?"

I groaned. "No. And that's all I'm saying. Do you want a drink?"

Mason released a sigh. "That would be fantastic. Shifting takes a lot out of me." He found a spot on my sofa and made himself comfortable, placing a cushion behind his back.

"Do you shift often?" I gathered two glasses out of the dining room. When I was in his apartment, he had been drinking scotch. I poured us each two fingers.

"Only in my apartment." Mason took his glass. "Because of the ban."

"Does it hurt?"

"It's not comfortable, that's for sure."

"Why do you shift at all, then?"

"It allows me to turn off my brain. It's very relaxing."

"You just lay around like that?"

Black's gaze was soft. He graced me with a gentle smile.

"I find a corner of carpet and curl up. I need to keep my wolf contained in my apartment."

"You'd hunt otherwise?"

"It would be difficult to stop myself."

That statement made my stomach flutter. Mittens and Carlos were my whole world. It sounded as if it had been hard for Mason to keep from hurting my cats.

He'd fought the urge to kill them.

For me.

"I can never repay you for bringing my cats back to me safely. Without you, some animal might have picked them off." Without thinking, I sat on the sofa beside him.

He looked me up and down.

I could see his chest rising and falling dramatically.

My cock stirred.

I raised my attention from his chest to his eyes. They were glistening, bottomless pools of molten emerald. At this distance, I could see they were flecked with gold and amber.

"I know how much they mean to you," he said softly.

"They're my family." I broke eye contact with Mason and took a sip of my drink. I embraced the warmth that unfurled in my stomach. Maybe it would calm me.

"I know you're feeling what I am," Mason said and set his glass on the coffee table.

I tucked mine closer to my lips, breathing in and out of the glass like a child trying to avoid the inevitable. I wasn't sure I was ready for this. Whatever *this* was.

"Your scent changed," Mason continued, then rose to his feet. "I should go."

I lowered the glass from my lips and onto my lap. Had I read the signals wrong? The way he had stared at me. I had convinced myself Mason was going to kiss me.

He was—wasn't he?

Why did he stop?

I stayed seated, confused, as he rolled down his sleeves, put on his suit jacket, and tucked his tie into his pocket. Then he was gone, and I was left wondering.

What almost happened?

Chapter Five | Mason

This shower wasn't meant to clean me. This shower was meant to soothe me. My day had not unfolded the way I had expected. Last night, I'd been tied to my bed being fucked by a colossal human—tonight I'd been considering kissing someone for the first time in years.

I lifted my face into the spray.

I barely knew him—Arnie.

What I did know, I liked. He was an intelligent and intuitive investigator. He was passionate about his work—focused. He was organized and disciplined. And he could talk paint off a wall.

I smiled.

The grateful, relieved, and adorable look on Arnie's face when I'd brought him his cats had stirred something in me. Something that had been dead for a very long time.

Hope.

He'd made me feel hope.

That's not all he'd made me feel.

I soaped up my hand and lowered it to my cock. Slow and easy, the image of Arnie licking his lips as he studied me, firing me up. He'd *wanted* me. That much was obvious.

I didn't take guys like Arnie to my bed. It would mean something to him. I couldn't have it mean anything. I couldn't let something like a simple kiss drag me down.

I closed my eyes and imagined his lips.

God, they're perfect.

I could feel them around my cock.

Pure, sweet Arnie.

I braced myself against the shower wall, pumping my cock. Faster—faster. I grunted and jerked and painted the grey tiles. With each thrust of my hips, I thought of him.

He was too good for me.

Innocent and good.

I didn't deserve innocent and good. My world was filled with sinful and morally corrupt. When I'd first moved to Metro City, I'd been guiltless—trusting.

That had been stolen from me.

The day I met *him* had been one of the few sunny days in the city since I arrived. I was two weeks into my classes. I was optimistic about my future in law enforcement.

He had approached me as I sat in the study hall, looking to borrow a pen.

His eyes had been mesmerizing, all grey and smoky—and devious.

I think I fell in love with him that first day.

He had courted me. Catching little moments with me. Giving me small thoughtful gifts. Showering me with affection. One day shyly taking my hand as we walked through the park.

He was so perfect.

My heart had sung for him.

I sank onto the floor of the shower. Like Bryan, the first time my love had hit me, I had believed it was my fault. I'd been hysterical, out of control, after seeing him kiss someone else.

Unlike Bryan, it wasn't just a slap. My love had endeavored to teach me a lesson. That the kiss I'd seen meant nothing to him, and that I was delusional for believing it to be more. That I was a needy little bitch looking for a correction. That I had brought the beating on myself.

Afterward, he'd broken down, sobbing—apologizing. He'd told me he loved me and would never hurt me again. That he was an idiot and so sorry for laying his hands on me.

And he'd kissed me until my tears stopped.

Touched my face. Stroked my hair. Held me in his arms.

It was another three months before it happened again.

I rolled against the shower wall, my body shaking as I sobbed.

He'd taken my innocence.

I wouldn't be taking Arnie's.

On autopilot, I climbed from the shower, opened the app on my phone, and searched for a *wolfmaster*. I was ready for him when he arrived.

A hulking human that looked nothing like Arnie. I closed my eyes, clenching and unclenching my fists, my wrists bound, as he pounded me into the mattress.

I let myself fly into the oblivion, my mind no longer dwelling in the past.

When he left my apartment, I slept.

Thinking of Arnie.

The next morning came too soon. I wasn't prepared to face my partner. After I'd left him wondering. After I'd let someone else fuck me. I dropped my toothbrush back in the glass.

Arnie wouldn't do something like that.

Fuck me.

It was too vulgar.

If we ended up in bed, it would mean something.

I didn't know how to process that.

I pulled up outside his apartment building. I'd texted Arnie to tell him I would pick him up at home. No point in both of us driving to the station and fighting to find a parking spot.

He slipped into the passenger seat and slammed the door.

"Good morning, Black."

Ouch.

That hurt, his reverting to my last name.

What did you expect?

I had turned him down last night. He'd been ready to take a leap with me, and I had shut him down. I suspected Arnie wasn't even gay. His attraction and desire for me had been building all day yesterday. His scent had slowly changed. From simple interest to attraction to arousal.

I turned to face him.

"Look, Arnie … what almost happened last night … can't."

Arnie chewed on his bottom lip and looked straight out through the windshield.

"You said you felt it too," he said finally.

I had to fight tears from forming in my eyes. It would have been beautiful. Taking Arnie to his bedroom and encouraging him to explore. To kiss him. To breathe up into his gentle tentative hands, to hear the sounds of his sighs—and have him fill me with his seed.

"I did—I do."

Arnie spun to face me. "Then why did you leave?"

There was only one answer. "I'm broken. I've forgotten how to simply be me."

Arnie didn't like that answer. He turned back away from me and crossed his arms. "Can we go? We have a lot to do today."

"Okay. We'll swing by the morgue first." Arnie was right. It was best if we immersed ourselves in working the case. Try to forget last night ever happened.

I hated the morgue. The scent of decomposing flesh filled my nostrils as we pulled up to the building. Being inside was so much worse. We didn't speak as we waited for the coroner to pull the body from the refrigeration unit. The silence, not having Arnie fill the space with the sound of his voice, made me uneasy. I contented myself with finding and holding onto the scent of him.

The coroner rolled the gurney over to us and uncovered the body. All the blood that had painted his throat and chest was gone. The wound was no longer red; instead, white and dead.

"Right from ear to ear," the coroner said, making a slicing motion with her finger. "He would have bled out slowly. His heart would have been working overtime, but the cold would have slowed the blood loss. Someone wanted him to die slowly."

"So, he was definitely alive when his throat was cut," Arnie stated.

"Alive and likely conscious. The sedative, a Rohypnol derivative, that was in his bloodstream would have incapacitated him but not knocked him out."

"Someone wanted him to feel the terror of dying," I said. "It was personal."

"Unlikely it was the people he owed gambling money to," Arnie added.

"There's a level of passion in a killing like this," the coroner said.

"Do you think Mitchell could muster a surge of hatred like this?" Arnie asked. "Yes, he lost his job in part due to Rockford's case but killing him like this is a bit extreme for that."

"I have a few more questions for Mitchell," I replied.

Arnie leaned closer to the body. "Me too." He pointed at a hand. "Can I see his fingertips?"

The coroner lifted Rockford's hand with gloved fingers and turned it over, palm up. Arnie inspected the fingertips, his eyebrows raised. "That's bizarre."

"Not having to wear gloves, he could feel the subtle clicks when cracking a safe," I said.

"There are latex gloves thin enough to do that," Arnie replied.

"It was a source of pride for him. Made him a novelty. I think he liked that."

"The bragging about no fingerprints," Arnie recalled.

"The theft cases … they tried to collect DNA from the tumblers."

"I know. I read the reports—inconclusive. A light touch."

"There are a few bruises that appeared after the initial exam," the coroner said. She lifted one arm. On the inside of his bicep was the imprint of what looked like fingers. "Both sides."

"From someone dragging him," I said.

"He would have been an absolute dead weight," Arnie added.

"Our killer is strong." I nodded at the coroner. "Thank you."

"One thing before you go," the coroner said. "I called the brother, Benedict. Told him I'd like him to identify the victim's body. Asked if he wanted to arrange a viewing. He declined."

That was strange. He had seemed adamant yesterday about seeing his brother. What had changed his mind? Didn't want to see his own face on a dead body? I knew I wouldn't.

"We'll be talking to him again today," I replied. "We'll follow up on that."

"We should go there first," Arnie said. "I like him for the killer better than Mitchell."

"Agreed."

I sucked in a massive breath of *different* air once we left the building. The air wasn't mountain fresh, but it didn't feel like it was burning the hairs off the inside of my nose.

I would have sneezed a few times if Arnie hadn't been in the car with me. Many of my habits were wolf-like. No amount of living among humans would change that. And I wouldn't want them to change in any way. I loved that I had a wolf in me. I was proud of my heritage.

We had to wait to see Benedict. He was out of the office. Half an hour passed until he showed up. His receptionist had called him back from a lunch meeting.

My stomach grumbled at the thought of food. I hadn't fed in days.

Finally, with Benedict, I held my tongue and let Arnie take the lead.

"You have no fingerprints. Is that true?" Arnie began.

Benedict looked at his hand. "Neither did our sire or grandsire. Genetic defect."

"You were in the military."

"Six years."

"Did you learn to repel and ascend?"

Benedict hesitated. "Yes, that was part of my training. Is that how they got in the hotel room?"

"We're simply exploring options at this point."

Arnie drew his lips to one side of his face in thought. I suspected where he was going next.

"Did you know about Rockford's arrangement with Daniel?"

"Daniel?"

"A concierge in the hotel. You went to high school with him."

"Don't remember him."

"You've never made use of the room's *amenities*?"

Benedict's jaw jutted forward. Wow, he had. He'd pretended to be Rockford and stayed in that hotel room. Partaken of the service offered by Daniel. I couldn't keep quiet any longer.

"You've met Daniel in that room and let him think you were Rockford."

Benedict grunted. "A few times. A while back, I wanted to take advantage of the spa in the hotel. Get a massage. Have a steam. Relax. I decided to stay over. Daniel didn't even ask me to sign in. Just handed me the keycard. Later that night … he showed up at my door."

"And did what?" Arnie asked.

"Pushed me into the room, shut the door, and dropped to his knees."

"You were surprised," I said.

"Figured out pretty quick that he thought I was Rockford. I let him think that."

"Was he hostile about it?" Arnie asked. "The *act*?"

A deep furrow appeared across Benedict's brow. "No, he was into it. Asked to kiss me afterward. Wanted me to hold him in bed until his break was over. Offered to come back."

Arnie and I looked at each other. Daniel had lied to us. His meetings with Rockford weren't under duress. The story about blackmail might not even be true.

Crime of passion.

Maybe Rockford had threatened to end their arrangement.

But was that reason enough to kill him?

What if Daniel loved Rockford? And he didn't want anyone else to have him.

One last thing.

"Why did you decline the opportunity to view and identify your brother?" I asked.

"Simple. I don't want to see what I'd look like dead."

"Understandable," Arnie said. "Well, I think that's all for now." He peered over at me. "Black … any more questions?"

"No, I'm good."

The ride down in the elevator to the parking garage was awkwardly silent. We had things to discuss to do with the case. What happened last night was interfering. I couldn't have that.

"Can we please move on?" I said as the elevator doors opened.

No answer. Halfway to the car, Arnie grabbed my arm and stopped me from proceeding. Normally, I would have recoiled from his touch, but this wasn't affectionate contact.

I drew my gun in unison with Arnie.

There was movement near the front of my car. So many humans and some wolves had been through the parking garage so far today, I hadn't picked up on anything unusual.

We both jumped back, relieved as a bird fluttered out from around my car. A falcon. In its talons, a poor unfortunate rat. The scent of a fresh kill filled my senses.

My stomach complained again.

"Do you mind if we stop somewhere so I can feed?" I asked.

"Like where?"

"A butcher. There's one near here." Maybe that was the answer. Let Arnie witness me tearing into a hunk of raw flesh. Remind him that I'm a wolf.

I exited the underground and headed down the road to where I had picked up meat before. I frequented the shop enough that the butcher knew me. Commented on my appetite for meat.

It was a quick trip in and out. After finding a secluded alley, I unwrapped the butcher paper against my steering wheel, salivating as the scent of bovine blood curled around my senses.

I shot a glance at Arnie, a brief warning as my canines descended. I peeled my lips back so he could see the fierce points as my pupils dilated and my fingernails lengthened.

He sucked in a breath and held it, not taking his attention off me.

He'd taken the same stance as I'd shifted last night. Up until he almost threw up. Even through the agony of shifting, I had smelled the rise of his bile.

Feed.

I turned back to the bloody steak, lifted it in one hand, saw red, and set about shredding and swallowing the tender flesh. I heard Arnie gasp and then nothing. The world fell away other than my detection if someone was to come too close to me. I would instinctively protect my *kill*.

Arnie kept his distance.

I swallowed the last piece of meat, and my awareness became clearer.

No.

The scent of Arnie's arousal surrounded me. With palpable apprehension, I looked at him. His eyes were smoldering with desire. My plan to put him off had produced the opposite effect.

No.

I shifted in my seat as my cock responded. My entire body tingled, buzzing. I was close to tears when Arnie raised his hand and cradled my jaw. My mind screamed at me to escape his touch. That it held no true meaning. That he was trying to appease me into submission.

Tears ran down my cheeks, mixing with the blood on my lips.

Arnie wouldn't do that to me.

I nuzzled my head against his touch, closed my eyes, and whined quietly. My mind became wrapped in a warm, long-lost blanket of pure innocent yearning. It felt good.

I was safe with Arnie.

"Who hurt you?" Arnie whispered as he brushed his thumb across my cheek. He shifted closer, his ass on the edge of his seat. "I promise, I'll never hurt you."

"Hurt is all I know," I said after a long silence. "I've never escaped years of hurt."

"Jeezus, Mason … let me show you something more." Arnie pressed his forehead to mine. "I want to show what it feels like to be truly cherished and respected. Not hurt—never ever hurt."

His hot breath—his promise. Every pure part of him, I chased it. His strong hand guided me to his lips. There was a moment of hesitation—a futile twisting in my mind, then I felt them. The lips I had dreamed of last night in my sleep, caressing mine—perfect and sweet.

Then I panicked.

When *my love* had first kissed me, it had been perfect and sweet.

It had turned ugly and demanding.

I yanked myself away from Arnie and shoved him.

"Whoa. Whoa." Arnie held up his hands. "Too fast. I'm sorry."

"You have no idea what I've been through."

"You're right, I don't, but maybe someday, you'll trust me enough to tell me."

I whined. I wanted to be there with him—ready to tell him. "I *do* trust you."

"As your partner on a case … or as a potential lover?"

I knew which I wanted—both.

I reached across the console for his hand. He smiled shyly at me, entwined my fingers with his, and clung to me. He leaned his head on his headrest and gazed into my eyes—trusting.

We'd need to trust one another.

"Only when you're ready," he said.

"Give me time."

"All the time you need."

I crossed the distance between the two seats and took another taste of his lips.

There it was again.

Hope.

"We need to get back to work," I said and kissed him again.

"Mitchell or Daniel?" Arnie ran his forefinger across my bottom lip, our lips nearly touching. His affection soothed me. I never thought I'd feel this way again.

I cleared my throat. "Daniel. He lied to us. I think he was in love with Rockford."

"Or who he thought was Rockford." Arnie moved back in his seat and adjusted his seatbelt.

I fired up the car and leaned for the glovebox.

Arnie popped it open. "What are you looking for?"

"Wipes. My face and hands are sticky with blood."

Arnie retrieved the box and handed me a square packet. "Suppose I need one too."

"Sorry about that."

"I know what I'm getting into."

I smirked as I cleaned my face. "Oh no, you don't. That was a polite feed."

"Oh, yeah?" Arnie tossed a wadded-up dirty wipe at me, then leaned toward me, and whispered, "Can those fangs of yours do anything else?"

His voice was so sexy and sultry.

It caught me off guard.

My already thickened cock pulsed.

"I'm going to drive the car now. Try to behave."

Arnie laughed and eased away from me. The rest of the day was going to be agonizing. I wasn't sure what the plan was when we ended our day, but it would need to wait.

We called ahead. Daniel wasn't working at the Grand Metro today. We were given his home address. He lived in a housing complex on the other side of the city from Arnie's.

It looked the same.

Same towers. Same parking lot and concourse. Same unsavory characters hanging around.

Same panicked response when I growled at them.

A flash and flicker of movement to my left caught my wolf's attention. My head whipped around, and my pupils dilated. My nostrils cleared themselves and I inhaled. *Daniel.* Hunt mode kicked in. On the third-floor exterior hallway, a figure running at top speed to the staircase.

I pointed. "Daniel—there."

Arnie had no chance of keeping up with me as I tore across the concourse. Daniel thundered down the staircase and leaped out through the door at the bottom.

I was on him.

He came crashing to the ground in a screaming heap as I tackled him, snarling and snapping in his ear. I didn't hear his words. Just that he kept struggling. My temptation was to bite into his throat to stop him from moving around. I had more control over myself than that.

"Stop!" I shouted at him past my descended canines. "My wolf *will* bite you!"

"Please, don't," Daniel screeched. "I'll stop. I'll stop."

My captive went limp beneath me as Arnie caught up to me, panting.

"Jeezus, you can move," he said, laughing as he propped his hands on his knees to catch his breath. I jerked Daniel around until I had him lying on his stomach. Arnie stepped in to assist me, removing a set of handcuffs off his belt. He placed his knee between Daniel's shoulder blades to immobilize him as I cuffed him. Once we had him secured, we lifted Daniel to his feet and walked him back to the car. Without a single complaint, Daniel slid into the backseat.

Arnie turned in his seat, facing Daniel, as I drove back to the station.

"Daniel Richardson," he said. "I'm placing you under arrest for the murder of Rockford Tennet. You have been promptly informed of the reason for your arrest as is your right. You have the right to retain and instruct legal counsel of your choosing. If you cannot afford legal counsel, an attorney will be assigned to you. And lastly, you have the right to remain silent when questioned. Do you understand your rights as they've been explained to you?"

"I do," Daniel whispered.

"Good." Arnie turned back to face the windshield. "Why did you run?"

"No comment."

"Oh, come on, Daniel," Arnie said. "We're trying to help you here. We know you were in love with Rockford. Why in the world would you want to kill him? You wouldn't, right?"

"No comment."

"Fine," I said. "We'll do it your way. Just remember, we tried to help you."

I inhaled deeply to explore Daniel's scent further. It had registered in my mind when I tackled him. I hadn't been sure the last time we interviewed him. Now, I was. Among all the scents that had been in the suite when I attended the murder, Daniel's had been there.

The entire bullpen stood as we hauled Daniel past their desks and into an interview room. Arnie locked him to the table with his cuffs, and we left him alone to stew.

"Okay," I said to my group of officers. "We've brought Daniel in but that doesn't mean we stop searching for other connections." I looked at Maxwell. "You interviewed the couple who were staying in the other room beside the victim's. And the people above and below."

"Dead ends. They don't have any intersection with Rockford's life. I'm satisfied we can discount them from further questioning."

"Send me what you have."

"Yes, sir."

I took Arnie aside. "He was there—Daniel. In the suite that night."

"How do you know?"

"His scent was there. So were almost ten other people's, plus the smell of the blood. I almost missed it. The entire scene was a slurry of scents. It was difficult to tell one from the others."

"You're sure?"

"Positive." I squeezed Arnie's shoulder. "You ready?"

"Yeah, let's see what we can get out of him."

Daniel was sufficiently wound up when we entered the room. He was fidgeting and sweating. Arnie and I took seats across from him.

"Did you know it wasn't always Rockford you were kneeling for?" I asked.

Daniel's eyes widened. "What?"

His breath hitched after he spoke. This was brand new information for him.

"Sometimes his twin brother, Benedict, came to visit you," Arnie said.

"Oh, my God." Daniel slumped in his seat, deflating. "I knew something was up."

"Why?" I asked.

"These past few weeks, he was more attentive and kinder. Actually open to holding me afterward. He'd never wanted to cuddle in bed before. He even showered me in kisses." Daniel looked at me, his eyes pleading with me for the truth. "Was that his brother, Benedict?"

"Most likely," Arnie said. "That night, though, Rockford was there."

"What was Rockford like the night of his murder?" I asked.

"We know you were in the room," Arnie said.

"I thought he was mad at me. He'd been so nice to me for weeks. That night, he was ugly again. Made me feel like an object to be used. I was devastated."

"So, you killed him," Arnie said. "Rappelled down from the roof and killed him."

Tears formed in Daniel's eyes as he shook his head. "No. I'd fallen in love with Rockford." He made a guttural whimpering sound. "I guess, I fell in love with Benedict."

"That would seem to be the case," I said.

Now that we had him in here, I didn't think Daniel had done it. There was none of the anger toward Rockford I would expect to see in him. A passion killing stuck with a killer.

His rage and aggression pheromones should still be off the charts. All I sensed was love.

And I was a sucker for it.

"Maybe Benedict would like to see you," I said. "He doesn't have a partner."

Daniel sat up straight in his seat. "Do you think?"

I shrugged. "He might. No harm in trying?"

"Am I not under arrest anymore?"

Arnie rose from his seat, walked around the table, and uncuffed Daniel. "No, you're free to go—for now. But be available for further questioning."

There were looks of confusion as Daniel walked back through the bullpen, a free man.

I waited until he was gone.

"We think he was simply lovesick for the victim," I said to the room. "I didn't sense he was the killer. He didn't have the chemical residue of someone amped up enough to have killed."

"Your wolf senses," Maxwell said.

"How reliable are they?" Linda asked.

"In this case—I think they're spot on."

"I agree with Black," Arnie said. "I'm not convinced Daniel had anything to do with the death."

"Who is contacting the climbing businesses?" I asked.

An officer in the back of the room raised his head. "No luck yet. One more store to go."

"Financial records for the new suspects?"

"Still working through them," Maxwell said. "Benedict's net worth is insane."

"Linda?"

"I'm tracking down friends and family of the suspects."

"Perfect. I'll leave you all to it." I put my hand on Arnie's back. "Jones. In my office."

I stepped through the doorway first and shut the blinds in the windows that overlooked the bullpen. Arnie closed the door behind him with his ass, his back pressed to it.

I tucked my bottom lip between my teeth as I approached him.

"Are you going to kiss me?" Arnie asked and smirked at me.

"I was thinking about it."

With my hands on his hips, I found a space between his feet and pressed my hard cock against him so he would know what he did to me. Arnie shuddered, almost lost his footing, and whimpered, wrapping his arms around my waist. "You can't *not* kiss me now."

I brushed my fingers across the unruly hair above his ear. "This is all new to you, isn't it?"

"With a man? Yes."

"We'll take it slow."

"Appreciated." Arnie's hands clung to my back and drew me closer. "But right now, I need you to stop talking and kiss me." One of his hands moved to my ass and tugged me to him.

He was rock-hard.

I groaned and sank onto his lips. Sighs of desire, our hands seeking, exploring, I slipped my tongue past his lips and into the warmth of his mouth. He tasted of coffee and cinnamon.

From around my waist, drawn up my chest, fingers digging into the hair at the nape of my neck, my unexpected lover undulated his hips against me. I felt as though I had fallen into an abyss. My only anchor, the man in my arms. I pinned him to the door and thrust against him.

He groaned quietly and thrust back.

We needed to bring this encounter to a close.

"We're going to continue this tonight," I whispered against his lips.

"Promise?" His fingers danced across my cheek. "You won't leave again?"

Never.

Then I said something that surprised me.

"I'll stay all night if you want me to."

"I want."

Sleeping over somewhere after having sex wasn't something I ever did. I reminded myself that sharing our bodies was going to mean something to Arnie.

I kissed him again.

I wanted it to.

Chapter Six | Arnie

I was floating when I left Mason's office. I'd never felt this way about anyone before in my life. He was the oxygen my entire being had been craving. I sat at my desk and lifted the cup with the picture of my cats on it. I had them to thank. Them and the cup. They had brought Mason to me.

He never would have ended up in my apartment if it wasn't for their existence. They were going to receive extra treats tonight.

Tonight.

I adjusted my collar to allow heat to escape. I was glad Mason had suggested we go to my apartment tonight. I wasn't sure how I'd react to being surrounded by bondage gear during my first time with a man. More heat prickled the skin right up to the height of my jawbones.

Would Mason expect me to partake in bondage someday?

I wasn't sure how I felt about that.

He left his office and walked toward my desk.

Looking so damned sexy.

"I want to finish ruling Mitchell out," he said to me.

"Let's go." I grabbed my coat.

In the car, the case was forefront in our minds.

"Do you think Benedict knows Daniel is in love with him?" Mason asked.

"Daniel has only known Benedict a few weeks. How could he be in love with him already?"

Mason looked over his shoulder at me, his eyes peering into my soul.

My heart stumbled.

Yeah—okay, I get it.

"Do you think Benedict loves him back?" I asked, pulling myself together.

"If he does, it gives him motive, knowing Rockford was having sex with Daniel."

"Did you detect Benedict's scent in the suite?"

Mason shook his head. "He and Rockford are identical right down to their cologne."

"I'm liking Benedict for this. I think he's in love with Daniel. He had to know how badly Rockford was treating him. He couldn't have been oblivious to the abuse charges from Bryan."

"Another question for Benedict."

"So, motive. Benedict is in love with Daniel and Rockford is likely being rough with him, maybe even abusing him. Rockford broke into his house and stole from him. And years ago, Rockford did something so heinous their mother disowned him."

"Maybe Benedict knows what it is. Maybe it's enough to make him want to kill his brother."

"Maybe." I retrieved my notepad and made some notes and sent them to the team, outlining where we were going with our discussion. "Means. He knows how to scale a building. He's strong enough to close the sliding glass door too hard. Especially if he was in a hurry."

"But the clothes. Why take them? And why leave the murder weapon behind?"

That I didn't have a theory for. "To send a message? He broke into your apartment that same night. Left you a useless clue to taunt you. This might be a game to him."

Mason slammed on his brakes, almost causing an accident.

"Jeezus!" He yanked his car off the road and screeched to the curb. "Has the coroner checked dental records for the victim yet? Confirmed Rockford's identity?"

I called up the coroner's notes. "She's still searching for the dentist."

Mason beat his hands on his steering wheel. "Stupid—stupid. I fucking missed it."

The light came on slowly in my mind. "The victim isn't Rockford, is it?"

"No, it's Benedict. Rockford is the ghost when it comes to break-ins, not Benedict."

I exhaled a long drawn-out, "Fuck."

We had assumed we had the right identity, even after learning Rockford had a twin brother. Rockford lived in the criminal world. A murder associated with that environment made sense.

We'd been talking to Rockford all this time.

Surely, his receptionist had noticed he wasn't up to speed with things.

"We need to talk to the receptionist," I said.

"Phone her. I don't want Rockford seeing us there."

I called Tennet Technologies and pressed the options to take me through to the private office of the president of the billion-dollar business.

A woman picked up.

"Benedict Tennet's office."

"Hi, this is Detective Jones. We've met a couple of times."

"Yes. I'll put your call through."

"No. No, don't do that. I want to speak to *you*." I switched the phone to my other ear. "The past couple of days, has Mr. Tennet been acting strange? Confused?"

"Actually, he has. He's usually on top of things but he's been … I don't know … floundering. I suppose that's to be expected with his brother being killed."

"I suppose. Thank you …?"

"Frances. Frances Littleton."

"Thank you, Frances."

I closed the call. "It's Rockford we've been talking to. Apparently, he's *floundering* at work."

"And has access to all that money. What do you want to bet, he tries to sell the company."

"He won't be able to keep up the ruse for long. He'd have to sell it."

"That's why there were no clothes in the suite. Benedict arrived dressed in one of his expensive tailored suits. If we found those clothes there, we might have put things together sooner."

"And the presence of the utility knife?" I asked.

"He was showing off. Rockford is all ego."

"Do we go arrest him?"

"He's not going anywhere. He wants *all* the money. We'll let him twist in the wind a bit longer, out of his depth in the business, while we gather some evidence."

"Daniel again?"

"Yes. He told us Benedict was cruel to him the night of the murder. That doesn't make sense. He hasn't told us the whole story."

I called the Grand Metro and confirmed Daniel was working. This time, he didn't run. It's possible he was living on the high that Benedict might want him.

He was going to be devastated.

We entered the privacy of a conference room.

I let Mason break it to him.

"Daniel, we have some difficult news to tell you," he said.

Daniel frowned. "What? Benedict doesn't want me?"

Mason sighed. "Rockford isn't dead."

"What?" Daniel burst to his feet. "But … the body."

The jagged puzzle pieces clicked together. When the last piece fell into place, Daniel broke down, crumpling into his chair, sobbing.

Seeing him torn apart like that pulled at my heart. He'd been in love.

His lover was dead.

"We need you to fill in some details," Mason said. "So, we can find Benedict's killer."

Daniel looked up, his face awash in tears, his nose running, and sucked in a short breath. I hoped this didn't destroy him. Falling in love could be a dangerous game.

I looked at Mason.

You barely know him. Too early to worry about losing him.

"Let's go over the night of the murder again," Mason said. "Everything this time."

"Walk us through the night down to the minute," I added.

Daniel nodded. "Rockford came in around 7 pm. I gave him the keycard same as always. Then around 8:30, I went up to the room."

"He was aggressive with you," I said. "During the blow job."

"Yes, but I assumed we'd curl up on the bed for a while after. He hit me for suggesting it even after I reminded him we'd been doing it for weeks. Reminded him we'd been kissing. That I thought we were building a relationship together. That I had feelings for him."

"I didn't see a mark on you," I said.

"He punched me in the gut. I thought he'd broken a rib."

"What happened next?" Mason asked. "When did the switch happen?"

Daniel's brow creased. "The one I thought was Rockford appeared at the desk an hour later. He was wearing different clothes. One of his suits. I thought he had nipped out for some kind of late meeting. He told me he needed to see me. He asked for a keycard which I thought was strange. I'd already given him one. Assumed he had lost it while he was out at his meeting."

"You went up to his room," I said.

"I know, I'm an idiot, but I did. He was distracted. I thought he was going to apologize for hitting me earlier. I sucked him off and left, feeling all kinds of dirty."

"That's why you didn't tell us about the second time," Mason said. "You were embarrassed?"

Daniel nodded.

"I'm sorry about Benedict," I said, and Mason and I stood. Daniel needed to be alone. I put a permanent marker through his name in my mind. He hadn't done it.

We walked down the hallway, leaving behind the sound of Daniel weeping.

"Mitchell again?" I suggested.

"Honestly, I'm done for the day. I'm satisfied that it's Rockford. Contact the team. Bring them up to date. Maybe they can start putting together some kind of case."

I slid into the car beside him. I wasn't sure how to bring it up. Whether he intended to go home to his apartment or come to mine with me.

"Your place?" Mason started the car.

A quiver ran through my stomach. That answered that question.

"If you're sure," I replied like an idiot.

Mason shut off the car. "You aren't?"

My heart thundered in my ears, nearly blocking out all other sounds. I was aware that my breathing had changed. I'd never been surer about anything.

Tell him.

"I want to be with you tonight," I said.

Mason leaned across the console, tucked my face into his hand, and kissed me.

"You can trust me," he said.

"I know."

Mason restarted the car and took his time driving to my apartment. I think he was trying to give me a few extra moments to think about what we were about to do.

I sighed and placed my hand on his thigh.

I was sure. I wanted this with him.

He wrapped his fingers around my hand as we drove. When we pulled into my parking lot, the usual crowd was absent from the door of the staircase. I was glad. It might be obvious I was nervous. Being alone meant I could cling to Mason's coat as we climbed the stairs.

This was unknown territory, but I was going to be exploring it with Mason.

The cats must have sensed something was up because they stayed on the sofa. My new front door closed, Mason slammed me against it and descended on my lips, his scratchy black stubble reminding me this wasn't a woman pinning me to the door. This was so much better.

Mason groaned and deepened the kiss.

He was hungry.

His fingers played with my coat and then peeled it off my shoulders. I danced through the next few minutes in a daze. Kissing—hands seeking. Clothes falling away.

Both bare-chested, cocks straining behind our pants, Mason grabbed my ass and jerked me toward him. I melted against him as he growled and played with my bottom lip in his teeth.

One hand on my ass, he used the other to pinch one of my nipples and drift down my chest—across my abs. I groaned and clung to his shoulders as he cupped and caressed my cock.

He breathed into my mouth, hitching his exhalations in unison with my faltering breath. I tipped my head to one side, his mouth skimming across my skin to my neck.

"Mason," I whispered as he kissed the sensitive spot behind my earlobe.

"My sweet Arnie," he whispered back.

My legs nearly crumpled at the sound of his voice. I wanted to experience every sound from him. I wanted to hear his voice as he came undone in my arms.

"Bedroom," I said.

Mason clenched my earlobe in his teeth, then, "Lead the way."

I moved past him, turned, hooked my fingers in his pant's waistband, and tugged him down the hallway, my lips parted as I kept eye contact with him.

His eyes were almost black.

When I backed up against the bed, I sat. His hard cock was so close. I gripped his hips. He ran his hands into my hair as I rubbed my cheek and lips on his shaft through the material.

His scent was strong. So male.

I kept my lips on his cock, looking up at him as I unbuttoned and unzipped his pants.

He stuttered through a breath but kept his attention on my eyes.

I was slow to peel his pants and briefs off his hips. I was met with a long thick cock. I released my hold on his pants and wrapped my hand around his shaft.

It was warm and velvety in my grip.

I stroked it a few times. A bead of precum formed at its tip. Desire surged through me, and I lapped at it. I closed my eyes and moaned as the pungent taste collected on my tongue.

Mason gripped a handful of my hair. I could tell he was fighting to stay still and let me take my time. I rose to my feet, changed positions with him, and pushed him onto the bed.

He lay back and I sank to my knees and finished taking off his pants.

I ran my hands up and down his thighs, thrilled by the abundant, bristly hair. I shuffled forward, pressed his cock to his stomach, and kissed his balls.

Mason swore and his hips rotated up, then settled back.

I was probably gentler than I needed to be. I used my other hand to lift his balls. I sucked one into my mouth. The hairs felt funny on my tongue as I rotated the sac around it.

Mason groaned and rearranged the placement of his feet on the floor.

I released his cock so it would rest on my face as I played with one ball and then the other. I liked the way his body enveloped me. I was sure my hair was sticky with his precum.

I inhaled and hummed as I moved from his sacs to his shaft. I wanted to immerse myself in his smell. I licked his entire length, holding his cock in my palm. At the tip, I sucked on his cockhead and ran my tongue around the thick ridge. Mason whispered my name.

I wanted to give him everything. I slid his cock along my tongue until it hit the back of my throat, then sucked it back to the tip. I smiled as I licked the cap. I was in heaven.

It was possible, I was gay.

I gripped the base of his cock and took him back into my mouth, this time wetting him with my tongue. I slurped and sucked until he sat up and touched my shoulder.

"Take off your pants," he said. "I want to see you."

With shaky legs, I stood and made quick work of my pants. Mason leaned forward and kissed each of my bare hip bones, then pumped my cock. His lips parted—

Oh, Jeezus.

His mouth was so much more talented than mine. I clung to his shoulders as he drew me in and out between his warm lips. I placed one hand on top of his head, riding the bobbing waves.

Mason sucked upward until I was free of his mouth. He set a kiss on my stomach.

"Come on." He shuffled up the bed. I crawled the length of it after him. I didn't want to be separated from him. We became a tangle of arms and legs as I stretched out on him, our stiff and tight cocks trapped against our bellies. His lips were back on mine, our tongues reuniting. He wrapped his arms around me and clung to my ass. His hips came up in a slow undulation.

I groaned and thrust back, grinding, as his cock rose against mine. He invaded and occupied every sense and faculty I possessed. I never wanted anything else—ever again.

His mouth slid from my mouth to my neck, to an area halfway to my shoulder. He licked and kissed my flesh there, our bodies writhing like seductive waves in sync.

I shuddered and sighed, "Yes," while clinging to him, my body teased to the point of shattering release as his sharp fangs dragged over my skin. I clawed at his shoulders, frantic.

I wanted more.

I'm not sure of what. I just knew there was more.

"Please," I whimpered.

Mason rolled us, so he was on top. He changed his angle, thrusting against me, our cocks heating, the caressing back and forth—our escalation reaching dizzying levels.

I was the first to break. I clung to Mason, gripping his ass, and thrusting up against him as I crested, hollering from the depths of a consciousness I was barely maintaining.

I guided his lips back to mine, hands on his face, seduced by the sensation of his fangs on my tongue as I slipped deep into his mouth. He groaned, fighting against something, and his sharp wolf-length fingernails dragged down the flesh on my back. He appeared to refocus. The space between us slick with my cum, the motion of Mason's hips became a gliding rhythm.

He released my mouth as his body tensed.

Mason grunted, pumped his hips, jamming against me, and spilled, his body convulsing. He mewled sweetly. I felt it in my heart. Pulse after pulse joined mine as his body slowed in my arms. Spent, he looked down at me—his gaze gentle.

Then he threw his head back—and howled.

The eerie sound gave me shivers.

It also brought me intense pleasure and relief. I brushed my fingers along his throat, enjoying the vibration. I doubted a wolf would howl after bad sex.

Mason's song finished, he climbed off me, and lay beside me with his eyes closed. When he opened them, a tear escaped, and formed a rivulet, running down his face into his ear.

"Talk to me," I said.

"It's nothing. It's been a while since I had sex where I wasn't tied down."

"Do you prefer being tied down?"

Mason rolled to face me. He tucked one arm behind his head. "Not with you."

"Why not?"

He reached out and stroked my face. "Because you mean something to me."

My soul soared at those words. He meant something to me too. What we had done together meant something. I had explored an experience I had only ever dreamed about.

"I think I might be gay," I said.

The corner of Mason's lip lifted. I turned to face him. His eyes were beautiful in this light. The sun was setting, filling the room with a dimming golden wash. The rain had stopped.

"I know I am," he said.

"But wolves don't call it that, do you? Gay."

"No. It's a pairing the same as any other. It's nothing different or special."

I blushed as my next words formulated in my mind. "This felt special."

I was graced with a smile as bright as the sun. "It was."

"Tell me about wolf pairings." I was crazy curious. Unlike some of my friends, I had never had a wolf in my life before. I knew very little about them. Now, I'd slept with one.

"A typical pairing would be one Alpha and one Omega."

"Which are you?"

"An Omega."

"What does that mean to be an Omega?"

"It means I'm supposed to be subservient to an Alpha."

I didn't like that, but maybe that's why Mason liked to be tied up. There was something in him that needed to be under someone's control. I couldn't see it—he was too confident.

"What would be *not* typical?"

"Sometimes an Alpha will take on a second Omega. I know a throuple like that. Declan, Patrick, and Tyler. The three of them are in love. They have five pups together."

Um ... what?

"Those are all guy's names."

"Omega males can become pregnant."

"Whoa … back up." I touched his chest. "*You* can get pregnant?'

"I can. My body is designed for it, but I'm on birth control."

"How do you … pregnant?"

Mason smirked. "Well, class … the sperm travels up into the uterus and fertilizes the egg."

"Ha. Ha. Could I get you pregnant?"

Mason shook his head. "No, we're not the same species."

That was a bit of a mind fuck. Not the same species. He looked like me. Maybe attractive on a mythical level. And his body was perfection. But that just might be the way I saw him.

"What about an Alpha and an Alpha?"

"Frowned upon. But I know another throuple that functions that way. Bryant, Greyson, and Hunter. Bryant and Greyson are Alphas. Hunter, their Omega. They've had a mess of twins."

"Are twins common?" This question related to the case.

"More common than in humans."

"Two Omegas?"

"They happen but they can't produce pups. Adding to the pack is important. We were hunted to near extinction many decades ago. Some packs never recovered. My pack, East Creekside, is thriving. My protectors alone had twelve pups. My brother Maddox is the leader now."

"Protectors?"

"Parents. I have a sire and a carrier. Both males."

"Carrier?"

"The wolf that carried and whelped me."

"That blows my mind that you can carry a … pup? Does it come out looking like a wolf?"

Mason laughed. "I can't imagine whelping a human-sized baby through there."

"Oh." Of course, it would be a rear exit situation. I had a hard time picturing that. I wasn't sure I wanted to picture that. A furry wolf being pushed out by Mason.

"Are pups able to shift right away?"

"Not until they're five. Then they stay that way in non-wolf form until they're around sixteen. At that point, they can shift back and forth freely."

"You spent your first five years as a wolf?" I couldn't imagine that. "What was that like?"

"I remember running around with my brothers and sisters having fun."

"You were close in age with your siblings?"

"Gestation is only 8 weeks. And my protectors were particularly amorous."

"So, a house full of wolf pups creating havoc."

Mason smirked. "My carrier, Adam, is patient in the extreme. He stayed home with us."

"My mom had to work."

"You have no siblings?"

"No. It was just us. My dad abandoned Mom and me when I was two."

"That must have been hard."

"It was the drug use that was hard. Mom couldn't keep a job. We typically lived off money from the city social program. Sometimes I wouldn't see her for days."

"Made you independent."

"Had to be. Learned to cook at an early stage. Get ready for school on my own."

Mason gripped my chin, came close, and kissed me. "I'm sorry you had to go through that."

I wanted to know why our first kiss had precipitated such an abrupt reaction. He'd pulled back from me, panicking as if our kissing had brought on a horrific memory. I knew not to ask.

"Tell me about where you grew up," I said.

"Creekside Township. The picture of a sleepy little town. As soon as I shifted to wolf form for the first time, I left home. I was lucky to be accepted into a university in Metro City."

"I got a job at a fast-food restaurant as soon as I was old enough to work. It was the first time in my life I'd had regular meals. Without that, I wouldn't have grown to this size."

"I was wondering about that. You're as big as an Alpha wolf."

"Would I be an Alpha in your world?"

Mason licked his lips, then bit his lower one. He nodded.

"And you'd be my Omega," I whispered.

Another nod.

"Would it turn you on if I called you my Omega?"

My cock pulsed.

Mason growled and closed the distance between us—fast. He brought our bodies together as he devoured my mouth, his need for me stunning my senses.

"Shower," Mason said.

That sounded like a good idea. I was all over the possibility of soaping up his entire body. Holding him in my arms. Kissing him into oblivion beneath the spray.

In the bathroom, I started the shower setting in the tub. There wouldn't be much room, but I suspected we'd be occupying the same space. I was right. Mason pushed me against the bathtub wall and continued his assault on my lips, his hard cock grinding against mine. He spun us slowly, so his back was against the wall. Then he turned so I was behind him.

I plastered my body on his, kissing the tantalizing length of flesh between his neck and his shoulder. It brought the memory of Mason dragging his fangs over that area on me to my mind. I growled thinking about it. He moaned and tipped his ass back. I ran my cock between his ass cheeks, thrusting, up and back on his skin. My eyes nearly rolled back it felt so good.

"Fill me," he whispered.

An unprecedented desire furled into a coil in my gut.

"Are you sure?"

"I want your seed in me."

Fuck.

That was hot.

I wrapped one arm around him to hold him steady, the other down between our bodies.

"I don't have lube," I said.

"We don't need any. My body produces something similar when I'm aroused."

"Mmm … good." I circled his hole with my cock, fascinated by the resistance. It took some effort to push past his ring. Mason moaned and reached back, holding his ass cheeks open.

I set my teeth against the area down from his neck as I thrust higher.

"Yes, Alpha," Mason mewled. "Harder."

The words fired up an inferno in my gut. I slammed the rest of the way into him. He pushed back against me and groaned. His hands slapped on the tiles. I moved both my hands to his hips and withdrew, then slid home again. I set a steady rhythm, rocking him against the wall.

Oh, my God.

The feel of his body around my cock, so tight—so soft. I wanted to exist solely like this for all time. He clenched and unclenched, and I almost lost my mind; I was so close to insanity.

Definitely gay.

I panted against him, wanting to be consumed whole by him.

He became my entire existence.

The sound of his sultry voice filled the small space. I buried my face against his hair, inhaling the scent of him. Drifted to the area at the top of his ear, the hard curl, kissing it. I brushed my lips back and forth, drilling him gently. I exhaled each time he grunted.

I kissed his neck. "My Omega."

"Fuck." Mason shuddered and his channel tightened hard around my cock. His body convulsed in my grip. Again—and again as he mewled and sighed softly.

I took hold of his cock, replacing his hand. It was spent, the tip coated in cum.

My words had done that.

"Such a sweet Omega," I whispered against his neck, increasing my pace. I wrapped my arms around his waist, holding him. I squeezed him tight as I thrust hard and filled him—.

With my *seed*.

I rocked my hips—in and out of him—slowly until I was too sensitive to continue. One last kiss on his neck and I slipped from his ass. He turned in my arms and took my mouth.

He needed reassurance. I could feel it in his desperation.

I broke our kiss and stroked his face. "You mean so much to me."

"Give me time."

I gathered him in my arms and set my lips on his head. "I can wait."

"I have a lot of crap to work through."

"I'm here for you." I grabbed the soap. "We really should clean up, then I can make us something to eat. I was going to cook a roast tonight. We can share it."

"I have a question first."

"What?"

"What's with the kid's comforter on your bed?"

I snorted. "When I moved to the primary bedroom, I couldn't get rid of it. I have a lot of memories of hiding beneath that comforter, blocking out the world."

Mason took the soap from me and started washing my abs. "You'd think those would be bad memories that you'd want to forget. The comforter must bring them back."

"I guess ... but it brings me comfort instead." I smiled. "My comfort comforter."

We took turns soaping each other up. My favorite part, running my fingers between his ass cheeks and washing the tight ring of his hole. He had let me in there.

I pressed my finger into it. Mason moaned and reached back for me over his shoulder, clinging to the back of my neck. Elated by his response, I sucked and nibbled on his ear.

My stomach grumbled.

Mason shook as he laughed. "We need to feed you. This is going to be a long night."

My cock pulsed hardening.

"Not until I fill you again, Omega. I want you dripping with me."

Mason whined, nearly melted, and put his hands on the wall.

It took us a while to get out of the shower.

Chapter Seven | Mason

I sat at the table in Arnie's small kitchen as he fussed about over at the counter. To save time, he'd cut his half of the roast into strips for him to cook. The other half, raw cubes for me.

Arnie looked adorable only wearing his briefs.

I wasn't used to waiting to eat. My canines had descended and wouldn't go back. Arnie had insisted we should eat together. I had to be patient while his strips of roast and the accompanying potatoes and carrots were cooked. I wrinkled my nose. The smell of vegetables was unpleasant.

The black cat came up to me and rubbed its body against my bare leg.

"Which one is this?" I reached down and petted it.

Arnie looked over his shoulder. "That's Mittens."

That made sense. Her little feet were white. Mittens purred as I scratched her head, then she must have caught sight of my fangs because she hissed at me and ran away.

"I think I scared her."

Arnie set the spoon down he'd been stirring with and came over to the table. He hauled my chair until I was facing the room, and sat, straddling my thighs. He held my face and brushed my lips with his thumbs. I gasped and my cock jumped as Arnie ran his thumbs down my fangs.

"I think they're sexy," he said. "Reminds me that you're dangerous. I like dangerous."

"You're an unusual human."

"You like me unusual."

He was right. I did. Arnie wasn't like anyone I'd met before. He was gentle but powerful all at the same time. The way his voice had curled around the word *Omega* had rocked me.

It had affected me differently than every wolf who had ever called me that. And there had been plenty. Alphas, Betas, and Omegas. Tying me down, flogging me, and calling me Omega.

Said in a way to put me down.

Arnie had said it with genuine affection. He cared about me. I was more than an object to be used. Prior misuse had been my fault. I always made it very clear, I just wanted to be fucked.

And left alone.

I was the epitome of a lone wolf.

My mind flitted to when *my love* had called me Omega.

I forced the painful memories out of my mind.

"When we were in bed together," Arnie started and went back to the stove, "and your fangs were down. You were dragging them across my skin. You seemed focused on one area."

"Your claiming area."

Arnie turned, the spoon in his hand. "My what?"

"When wolves find their chosen or fated mate, they claim each other by biting one another there. It's in my DNA to be attracted to that area when I'm having sex."

"I've heard about chosen or fated. You can't resist your fated mate, right?"

"The pull to be with them is too strong to resist."

"What if you don't like them?"

I grinned at Arnie. "That's all part of it. You like them. Eventually, you fall in love with them. Fate chooses a mate who matches you perfectly. It's a good thing, Arnie."

"And chosen?"

"Sometimes a wolf will find someone they fall in love with even though they're not fated. That wolf becomes their chosen mate. They claim each other like they're fated."

Arnie turned his back to me. "Are chosen mates ever human?"

My gaze wandered over his strong shoulders.

God, I hope so.

"My Uncle Jonas has a human Alpha mate. Damon has wolves somewhere in his ancestry. They were able to get pregnant. Their daughter is essentially human. She can't shift."

"So, a human *did* get a wolf pregnant."

"Rare." I squirmed in my seat. "Do you want children?"

Not sure why I asked that.

"With the right person, sure." He clicked off all the heat elements on the stove. I was so ready for the food. Anything to close where I had taken the conversation. I didn't want pups.

"You?" Arnie asked.

Dammit.

"My life isn't set up for pups," I replied. "My bedroom alone would be a problem."

Arnie set our plates on the table. His was steaming. Mine was bloody.

"What do you get from it … the bondage?" He cut into his cooked roast. I looked at my raw cubes. I hobbled my senses. I could only resist for a few seconds before I saw red.

"It relaxes me. Turns off my brain. The closest thing to being in wolf form." I swallowed as saliva swamped my mouth. "Can we talk later? I can't resist the meat any longer."

"Sure. Go ahead."

I inhaled and let the surge overtake me. My canines finally had something to tear into. Arnie's kitchen disappeared. Using both hands, I ripped at the flesh, snarling and gulping.

I wasn't as neat this time. I didn't have a suit to protect.

My stomach full, I lifted the plate to lick every drop of blood off it.

My vision cleared. To my astonishment, Arnie had finished most of his meal. He'd continued eating as I'd been feeding. I excused myself and went to the bathroom to clean up.

After washing my face and hands, I looked at myself in the mirror.

What was I getting into with Arnie? I'd maintained a cage around my heart for so long that I wasn't sure I would be capable of someday handing Arnie the key.

If that's where we were headed.

I'd certainly let my guard down. I didn't kiss. I didn't let anyone touch me if there were any semblance of affectionate feelings attached. I'd let Arnie do both.

A soft knock.

"Are you all right in there?" Arnie asked.

"Existential crisis in progress."

"Anything I can help with?'

I pulled open the door and walked into his arms. "I need you to hold me."

"I can do that." He led me to the bedroom, guided me onto the bed, and tucked me against him, my back to his chest. He wrapped his arm around me and threw his leg over my thigh.

"Better?" Arnie asked and kissed the back of my head.

It must have been, because the next time I was conscious of my surroundings, there was light coming in through the window. A cloudy, rainy day … but some light.

I hadn't slept through the night like that in years.

Arnie hummed against the back of my head. "Good morning."

"I passed out. I'm sorry."

"You obviously needed the rest."

"What time is it?"

"Just after 6. We have time to shower and dress." Arnie's fingertips drifted up and down my arm. He shifted, prodding his hard cock against my ass. "Unless you don't mind being late."

I *so badly* needed to be late for work.

But we were in the middle of a murder investigation. We'd already knocked off early yesterday to spend some time together. I had to put on my detective-in-charge hat.

"I want to do this again ... but maybe tonight."

Arnie laughed. "You're no fun. I thought sleeping with the boss would gain me perks."

I smiled. "Sorry to disappoint. Unfortunate the perks are the only reason you did it."

Arnie growled and pulled me to him, squeezing me way too tight. "So untrue."

I played with his fingers. "What we did ... I don't usually do that."

"Make a connection with someone." Arnie's voice came out in a whisper as if he was unsure of what he was saying. I wanted him to know I was right there with him.

"We have two words in wolf language. Mating and rutting. Both words for having sex."

"What do they mean?"

"Rutting is like fucking. Meaningless sex for the purpose of gratification. That's what I always do with my sexual partners. What I've been doing for years." I kissed his hand. "Until now. What we were doing wasn't rutting. We weren't fucking for the sake of fucking."

Arnie buried his face at the base of my neck. I could feel his hot breath.

"What does mating mean?"

"Sex with affection and respect." I left off that mating was something that fated and chosen mates and mates in love did together, and that it was done with the intention of producing pups.

The human phrase would be *making love.*

"Were we mating?" Arnie asked. "I like to think we were, but it felt like more than sex."

Tears collected in my eyes, and I nodded. I'd felt it too. The connection Arnie had spoken of. We'd hurtled toward one another since we'd met. Last night, we'd finally slowed down.

I loved what I'd found in Arnie.

I wondered if we'd truly mate someday.

"We need to get up," I said.

"Yes, boss." Arnie rolled away from me and left the bed. A cold chasm opened behind me that was Arnie-shaped. The cutout went straight through my heart.

I lay there, listening to Arnie showering.

I needed more of his presence before we headed to work.

I wandered into the bathroom intending to climb beneath the spray and shower for work. It didn't turn out that way. I couldn't resist him filling me one more time.

At 7:30 am, we walked into the bullpen. There were a lot of frustrated expressions. We knew who the killer was, but we had no way of tying him to the crime.

I had suspected that would be the outcome.

"Dental report came in," Linda said. "It's confirmed, the victim is Benedict Tennet."

"Well, that's something, at least," Arnie said.

Everyone stood at once, silent, staring at the doorway to the hall. I spun around to see what the fuss was about. Arnie grabbed my sleeve.

Rockford Tennet.

Standing in our bullpen.

"Well, that ruins part of my surprise," Rockford said. "Knew you'd figure it out eventually."

Arnie hustled over to our board and flipped it over to hide what we'd been working on. Our main suspect did *not* need to know we had nothing on him.

"What are you doing here?" I asked.

"Thought I might tell you a little story … since someone thought they killed me."

"Not here," I said. "We need to tape this."

"Lead the way," Rockford replied.

Arnie ushered him along into an interview room. We could discuss Rockford's bizarre appearance in our bullpen once we heard whatever tale he was about to tell us.

I closed the door and took a seat beside Arnie.

Rockford leaned back in his chair across from us, grinning.

Cocky bastard.

I pushed play on the recorder. "This is Detective Black. I'm with Detective Jones and Rockford Tennet. It is …." I checked the clock. "0736."

Silence fell in the room.

"Start," Arnie said to Rockford.

"Right," Rockford said. "Where to start. I suppose I could begin with my frequent stays at Grand Metro. I've been finding refuge there for years. My money isn't exactly reliable. Thanks in part to my dear departed brother. At least he let me stay in the business suite."

He drummed his fingers on the table. "Can I have a glass of water?"

"Jeezus." Arnie shoved his chair back and left the room. He returned with a glass of water and practically slammed it down in front of Rockford.

"Tell us about Daniel," I said.

"Needy little bitch," Rockford said. "I wouldn't have figured out that Benedict was using him too if Daniel hadn't gone on about us kissing and holding each other on the bed."

"Benedict wasn't *using* Daniel," Arnie said.

I nudged his thigh with my knee to stop Arnie from going down a rabbit hole. Daniel's situation had upset Arnie. It had bordered on triggering for me.

We needed to remain impartial.

"The killer didn't realize Benedict was using the suite too," Rockford said. "Caught me by surprise, that's for sure, but this person thought it was me staying there."

"Who is this person?" Arnie asked.

Rockford waggled his finger at him. "Now, where's the fun in me telling you that."

"But you know who it is," I said.

"Someone who wanted me dead. They took a serious risk to end me."

Arnie leaned forward. "A risk? What kind of risk?"

"They risked giving themselves away."

Fuck.

I slammed my palms against the edge of the table. Rockford wasn't going to give us anything useful. "We know you killed your brother. You're making up fantasy stories."

"*Know*?" Rockford tipped his head to one side. "I somehow doubt that." He tapped his pointer finger in the middle of the table. "The killer left clues. You probably missed them."

"What kind of clues?" It was worth a shot.

"Small ones."

I burst to my feet. "Interview over." I reached down the table and turned off the recording.

"Don't you want to know why they did it?" Rockford asked.

I didn't bother turning the recording back on. This was all a load of bullshit.

"Enlighten us," Arnie said.

Rockford grinned. "Because I'm a nasty piece of work."

"We knew that already," Arnie replied.

Rockford inhaled slowly. "Does your staff know you're sleeping together?"

Arnie surged at Rockford and grabbed him. "Rockford Tennet, I'm placing you under arrest for the murder of Benedict Tennet. You have been promptly informed of the reason for your arrest as is your right. You have the right to retain and instruct legal counsel of your choosing."

Rockford struggled in Arnie's grasp. Arnie continued. "If you cannot afford legal counsel, an attorney will be assigned to you. And lastly, you have the right to remain silent when questioned. Do you understand your rights as they've been explained to you?"

"You can't arrest me … I'm Benedict Tennet."

"Shut it." I pulled my cuffs off my belt. "Do you understand your damned rights?"

"I do," Rockford said. "But I'll be out in a few hours."

"It'll give you time to reflect," Arnie said as he cuffed Rockford.

His hands cuffed behind his back; Rockford fought us as we tried to leave the interview room with him. "I want to speak to my lawyer." Arnie shoved him through the doorway.

Four of my officers took over. They would take Rockford down to booking. He would see a judge in a few hours—and be set free. We had no evidence against him.

The arrest was more about annoying him.

He'd wasted our time. I had a creeping feeling, though, that he was telling the truth. That he hadn't done it. That someone thought they were killing Rockford Tennet.

I flipped our bullpen board back over.

"Let's start again," I said to the room. "Every piece of evidence re-examined. Rockford has told us we missed something … and I'm inclined to believe him."

"Someone who has a reason to kill Rockford," Arnie said. "Dig."

"I want to talk to Mitchell Dunnigan again," I said to Arnie.

"Can I drive for a change?"

"My car? You want to drive my car?"

"I'd rather drive you," he whispered. "Crazy."

"That's the only thing you'll be driving. No one touches my car."

"See … there's that lack of perks thing again. I might have to rethink my sleeping arrangements." Arnie brought his shoulder to mine and lowered his voice. "My sweet Omega."

I had to turn away from the room. My cock had responded to Arnie's words in spectacular fashion. I thought of Creekside and the chores I'd been expected to do. Dusting—sweeping.

"You all right?" Arnie asked.

"Thinking about housework."

Arnie snorted. "Let's go. Get this interview with Mitchell over with. I want to strike him off our suspect list. You can drive … even though you seem to be easily distracted."

"When it comes to you—yes."

"I'm going to take that as a compliment."

I grunted and retrieved my coat. Arnie was waiting for me by his desk, sitting on the edge of it. He had an ease with his impressive body that I'd witnessed firsthand last night. I bit my bottom lip and smiled at him. We'd fit together like we were fated.

Arnie smirked when I threw him my car keys. He was easy with her. I was surprised he knew how to drive a stick shift. Most people had never even seen one.

Mitchell was a little surprised to see us at his door, but he ushered us into their apartment without question. We went through the same routine as last time, waiting for his wife, Cathy, to make us all tea and cookies. Arnie made quick work of two cookies again.

"You've told us you're financially strapped," I said.

"Yes," Mitchell replied. "Money is tight. The taxes and homeowner's fees on this apartment alone are astronomical. And you know what's happening with grocery prices."

I grunted. I had no idea. My usual butcher knew I was a wolf.

I scared him.

I got a deep discount.

"So, you do own this apartment?" Arnie asked.

"Yes, we sold our house," Cathy said. "Bought this apartment. We lived off the difference in investment for a while. Then I went back to school and requalified for nursing."

"Staying at the Grand Metro was a treat," I said. "How did you afford it?"

"Didn't cost us a cent," Mitchell said.

Now, that was a twist.

"Why not?" Arnie asked.

"We received a gift card by courier from the hotel."

"For a free room," I said.

"One night … all paid for," Mitchell replied.

"Were you able to pick the night?" Arnie asked.

"No, the night was set. Cathy had to book off work."

"And the room number?" I asked.

"That was set too."

"How much notice were you given?"

"Two days."

"Did the gift card say who it was from?"

"It was anonymous. A friend giving us a belated anniversary gift."

"It was your anniversary recently?"

"Two weeks ago."

I looked at Arnie. He nodded at me. It seemed the Dunnigans had been placed in our path to throw us off and take us down a useless line of inquiry. Other than determining the murder was planned. Coinciding with the Dunnigan's anniversary was on purpose.

Arnie stood. "Thank you. This will be the last time we bother you. You can go visit your daughter now. We don't need you to stay in the city anymore."

I extended my hand to Mitchell. "Thank you for cooperating with us."

"Pleasure to help the police. Hope you find the killer."

We left them alone to bask in the recognition of their innocence. We sat in my parked car in silence, thinking. We'd come to a lot of dead ends. We only had one person to go back to.

"We need to interview Bryan again," Arnie said. "As Rockford's abused ex, he has motive."

"Start the team working on him."

I'd been blind to it—the possibility that Bryan's love for Rockford might lead to murder. I couldn't imagine killing my abusive ex. He still had a vice grip on my heart.

As well as the bondage calming me, it helped drown out the memory of him.

I stared out the window at the wet city streets as Arnie drove us to the outskirts. The housing development was an hour further than that. We pulled up outside Bryan's house.

This time, he was the one to answer the door.

"I figured you might be back," Bryan said.

He led us through the house to a glass-paneled solarium. The patter of rain on the glass above was almost soothing. Metro City wasn't the place to be if you didn't like the sound of rain.

"We have more questions," Arnie said.

"Starting with where you were the night of the murder," I said.

"I was home all night. Got groceries around 7. Came home—stayed home."

"Can anyone verify that?"

Bryan shook his head. "No, Justin was staying at his sister's. She's been ill."

"Same bone condition?" Arnie asked.

"Yeah … most of the family has it. They struggle to have a normal life."

"Can we have her contact information, please?"

Arnie typed it into his notepad after Bryan found it in his phone.

"Tell me, Bryan, do you enjoy recreational climbing?" I asked.

"Climbing?" His brow furrowed at me. "No, I've never tried it. Not sure someone of my size would find climbing very easy."

"It only takes you to be fit," Arnie said. "Size doesn't matter. You seem fit."

"Like I said—I've never tried it."

"So, you won't mind if we have a team search your house."

Bryan shook his head. "No. Go ahead."

Arnie typed on his screen, likely starting the process of a search warrant.

"Did you hate Rockford?" I asked.

Bryan sighed and looked toward the doorway to the room we were in. I suspected he was checking to make sure Justin wasn't within earshot.

"I still loved him," he whispered.

"How would you react if we told you he isn't dead?" Arnie asked.

Bryan's look of longing and hope was heartbreaking. Tears formed in his eyes, and he clutched the arms of his chair. "He isn't?"

"It was Benedict Tennet we found in that room," I said.

Bryan's body crumpled, falling forward, his hands over his face. The sound of his sobbing surrounded us, rebounding off the room's glass walls and ceiling.

I closed my eyes and steadied my breathing.

Few understood the addiction component of staying with an abuser. I'd hated and loved him at the same time. I *needed* him. At least I thought I did. He'd convinced me no one would ever want me. The day I'd packed a few clothes and checked into a hotel had nearly killed me.

Finally leaving my drug of choice behind.

My chest hurt as it tightened.

I'd almost gone back to him many times. He'd texted me the sweetest messages and had fields of exquisite flowers delivered to the station for me with loving handwritten notes.

One day, as a reluctant date, I'd let him take me to the art gallery.

He'd held my hand and told me how much he loved and missed me. It had taken all my strength to walk away that day and tell him not to contact me again.

The text messages after my decision turned vile, calling me a little bitch and a useless stupid cunt. It was then that I finally blocked his number. The flowers and notes stopped.

Now, he came to me in dreams two ways. Sometimes, he was sweet, showering me with love. Other times, I fought to consciousness, sweating, my heart thudding at a terrifying pace.

He'd been an undisciplined abuser. Pure rage. My face had taken the brunt of his anger. I still had thin white scars through my eyebrows where he'd punched me in the face so hard, my skin had split. I touched my face. He'd almost broken my nose many times.

The shame I'd felt walking into work each day had been extreme. I had covered up by saying I'd taken up boxing. No one questioned me. No one knew why I spent so much time at work.

Bryan was still sobbing. Part broken heart—part relief.

Arnie touched my sleeve.

"My arms are waiting to hold you," he whispered.

I gazed into his warm, caring brown eyes and nodded.

I was ready to tell him—everything.

"Bryan," Arnie said. "We need to finish this."

The room quietened as Bryan brought his emotions under control.

"Did you kill Benedict?" I asked. "Thinking he was Rockford."

"I don't want Rockford dead. I'd never want him to be dead." He shook his head. "There's this fucked up part of me that thinks he'll change."

"And you'd go back to him," I said.

Bryan hesitated. "No. I love Justin."

The right answer but he'd taken a moment to think about it. My heart ached for him. To be so conflicted despite one's history with the person. Bryan was right … it *was* fucked up.

My senses picked up Justin before he even entered the room.

Musty.

Damned birds.

"Everything all right in here?" he asked, then seeing the state of Bryan's tear-streaked face, he rushed to Bryan's side. His head snapped around and he glared at us. "What did you do to him?" He squatted at Bryan's feet and held his face. "It's all right, baby … I'm right here."

"Rockford isn't dead," Bryan said on a long exhalation.

Justin jerked to his feet. "What?" Again, he shot us a glare that could bore a hole in metal.

"It was Benedict Tennet who was killed," Arnie said.

"That can't be," Justin said. "You said it was Rockford."

"We hadn't checked the dental records yet. We were mistaken with the identity."

Justin's bony chest rose and fell fiercely—and fast. "So, you're positive now?"

"Yes," I said. "It wasn't Rockford who was killed."

Justin clenched his fists. Bryan had filled him in entirely on the abuses he had suffered at Rockford's hands. He'd believed his partner's abuser had finally received his punishment.

I looked at Arnie.

Arnie tipped his head to one side and shrugged.

"Justin, where were you the night of the murder?" Arnie asked.

"At my sister's." He put his fists on his hips. "What's this got to do with me?"

"Did you know Rockford sometimes stayed at the Grand Metro?"

"How on earth would I know something like that? Are you accusing me of the murder?"

"Rockford was violent with your partner," I said. "Did you want him dead?'

"Of course, I wanted him dead. Doesn't mean I tried to kill him."

"We're going to be checking your alibi," Arnie said.

"Go ahead. Check away. My sister has been having difficulty around the house. I head over there every couple of weeks to tidy up and stock her groceries."

"And you stayed over?"

"I always stay over."

"Convenient," I said, but that simple observation pissed Justin off.

His face twisted with fury. "Get out!" He pointed at the door.

We were finished anyway. We retreated after our standard *don't leave the city*. Justin had just landed himself on our board of suspects. He was too frail to lift a body the size of Benedict's but maybe he'd had help. We arrived back in the bullpen with a question.

"Can anyone tell me about the bruises that were found on the victim's arms?"

Maxwell raised his hand. "Big hands. The size of Benedict's."

I turned to the board. "Can we get a picture of Justin up here?"

"Is he a suspect now?" Linda asked.

"He hates Rockford for what he did to his mate, Bryan. Not sure how he did it, though."

"He couldn't have hired anyone," Maxwell said. "They filed for bankruptcy last week." Interesting information but I wasn't sure it was relevant other than Justin probably didn't have access to enough money to pay a hitman. Maybe he'd used the last of their credit?

"Check their bank and credit card statements, Maxwell. Deep dive on it, and make sure Justin doesn't have any secret accounts anywhere. Look for a large withdrawal."

"On it," Maxwell said.

I caught Arnie's attention. "Jones, in my office for a moment, please."

Near my breaking point, I closed my office door behind us and turned the blinds so no one could see us. Arnie held out his arms and motioned with his fingers, and I headed straight for him. Straight into the peace I knew I'd find there.

"I've got you," Arnie whispered as he held me and kissed my head. "I can't imagine how hard that was for you. Seeing Bryan like that. So viscerally relieved his abuser wasn't dead."

"He hesitated."

"When you asked him if he'd go back to Rockford?"

I nodded. "I've been there … many times."

"You've thought of going back to him."

Arnie had figured out how personal this was for me. That I had domestic violence in my past. That I shared a timeline similar to Bryan's.

"My heart tries to tell me it would be different this time," I said.

"You know it wouldn't, right?"

"My mind knows that. But even my mind falters sometimes."

"He's got a hold on you still."

"It's been almost five years since I left him. He still haunts my dreams."

"What can I do? Anything?"

I buried my face against the collar of his coat, whining, and inhaled the scent of his neck. I just needed Arnie to keep being Arnie. "Just keep being you."

Arnie's body shook with a gentle laugh. "That I can do."

I stepped away from him. "We can talk more later."

"Are you sure you're ready? We barely know each other."

"I know enough to know I want to open up to you."

Arnie cupped my face. "Fuck, you're fucking killing me." He lowered his lips to mine and my past melted from my mind. Arnie was everything I needed. Everything I wanted.

He was the only one who might chase my nightmares away.

I surged up into his kiss.

He was my Arnie.

And I was his Omega.

Chapter Eight | Arnie

Maxwell hadn't found any unusual activity on any of the accounts Bryan and Justin held, together or individually. It didn't mean Justin hadn't sold something to pay for a hitman.

I parked the car by the curb in front of Justin's sister's apartment building.

Lillian Samson. Never married. Living off a city disability pension.

Mason rang the buzzer.

"Hello?"

"This is Detective Black with the Metro City police department."

"What do you want?"

"We have questions about your brother."

Silence … but then the door buzzed to let us in.

I was very aware of the fact Mason wrinkled his nose as Lillian opened her door. I found myself looking at him a lot, my mind revisiting the shower, and the sounds he'd made as he'd cum. I sighed; my heart warmed. I hoped he'd come back to my apartment again tonight.

We were led into Lillian's small living room. Justin hadn't been very successful in keeping the apartment clean. The space bordered on a hoarding situation.

We found places on the sofa to sit after moving stacks of newspapers.

"We have questions about your brother," Mason reiterated.

"My brother is a good man."

I couldn't help staring. Lillian's bones were more visible than Justin's. Not just her hands and arms, but her clavicles and cheekbones. The effect was haunting.

"Your brother came to visit you recently," I said.

"Yes, he comes every couple of weeks."

"And he stayed overnight?" Mason asked.

"Yes, he always does."

"Did he stay in the apartment the entire night?" I asked.

"Is he in trouble?"

"We just need to know where he was that night," Mason said.

"He stayed here with me all night."

"You're sure about that?"

Lillian looked down at her hands. She was nervous. It seemed to be her constant state of being. I knew it wouldn't take much to push her into talking.

"Where did he go?" I asked, letting my voice drop an octave.

She fiddled with her skirt. "He went out."

"What time?"

"Around 11 pm. The News was just starting."

"Did he say where he was going?" I asked.

"He was meeting a friend for a drink."

I leaned forward. "What friend?"

"Someone named Frances."

Mason's eyebrows rose. This bit of information was unexpected. "Frances Littleton who works as a receptionist at Tennet Technologies?"

Lillian nodded. "Yes, that's the one."

"How long has Justin known Frances?" I asked.

"They met in college. Stayed in touch."

"How long was he gone?" Mason asked.

"A few hours. I fell asleep in front of the television. When he woke me to help me to bed, the 2 am cooking show was on."

Mason and I both stood.

"You've been very helpful," I said.

"One last question," Mason said. "Do you keep birds?"

Lillian furrowed her brow. "No, that's my brother's hobby."

"Then, that's it."

"Thank you," I said.

Away from Lillian's apartment, we raced through the rain and slung ourselves into the car. Mason was deep in thought. I let his mind percolate.

"That smell again," he said at last. "You can't smell it?"

"The musty smell? Yeah, a little. Pretty strong in that apartment."

"It's bothering me."

"You think it has something to do with the murder?"

"How could it?" Mason replied.

"I'll have the team make a note about a musty smell anyway."

Mason nodded. "We need to speak to Frances. She knew when Rockford was staying at the suite. She might have shared that information with Justin."

"So, we have motive and opportunity for Justin. But the means …?" I pulled out my notepad. "I'm adding DNA samples for Bryan and Justin to our search warrant. Bryan because I don't want to spook Justin. Maybe Justin will be in our database."

I eased the car into traffic headed for Tennet Technologies. We weren't the least bit surprised to find that Rockford was already back in his office. The jail process had been quick.

"No, we don't want to see him," I said to Frances.

"We need to talk to *you*," Mason said. "Can we go somewhere more private?"

"We can go to the break room." She led us there and set about putting on a fresh pot of coffee. I hadn't had enough of the elixir today. The scent of the grounds started a craving.

"How long have you known Justin Samson?" Mason asked.

"Since college. Why?" She poured water into the back of the coffee maker.

"Do you ever discuss work with him?" I asked.

"Just in passing."

"Ever mention that Rockford stays at the Grand Metro sometimes?"

"Yes." She added the coffee grounds and turned the machine on. "Justin had me keep track of how often and when Rockford stayed there."

"Why?"

Frances shrugged. "I thought Justin wanted to confront Rockford about his previous relationship with his partner, Bryan. There was some serious abuse."

The image of those bruises on Benedict's arms appeared in my mind.

Marks from hands the size of Benedict's.

"Does Benedict ever talk about his brother?" I asked.

Frances rolled her eyes. "I've never seen anything like it … the hatred."

Mason tipped his head. "Benedict hated Rockford. You're sure."

"I stopped telling him when Rockford was staying in the suite. To keep them separated."

"You were concerned for Rockford's life?"

"I've known Benedict for a long time. I've never seen him get so worked up. When Rockford broke into his house … stole all that stuff and sued him … Benedict was livid."

"There was another incident when Rockford was younger. Something that affected their mother so vehemently that she disowned Rockford. Do you know what that was?"

"No, sorry. I'm not *that* close to Benedict."

"Do you think Justin hated Rockford enough to kill him?" Mason asked.

Frances blinked at us a few times. "I wouldn't discount that possibility."

"You went out with Justin the night of the murder. Where did you go?"

Frances frowned. "I didn't. I didn't see Justin that night."

Justin's opportunity factor just jumped up. We needed to figure out how Justin had done it. And whether Benedict's hatred of Rockford had landed them both in the suite that night.

Maybe Benedict had gone there to kill Rockford.

But Rockford surprised him instead.

I needed to speak to Mason privately.

"Thank you, Frances," I said. "That's all we need for now. Don't leave town, please."

"Have I gotten Justin in trouble?"

"If he's in trouble, it's his own doing," Mason said.

In the elevator, we had a moment alone.

"I think Benedict went to that suite to kill Rockford," Mason said.

"I think so too."

"But when he got there, the suite was empty. Rockford had gone out."

"Daniel went up to see who he thought was Rockford, then left."

We emerged in the underground parking. "Rockford returned to the suite."

"Found Benedict there," Mason finished my thought.

"They shared a drink. Rockford slipped the Rohypnol in Benedict's drink." I opened the car door, slid into the driver's seat, and unlocked the passenger door for Mason. Something about that timeline didn't make sense. "Why did Rockford have Rohypnol in his possession?"

Mason sat, looking down at his hands. "He was going to use it on Daniel."

"Why in the world would he …?"

Jeezus.

Mason's ex had done the same to him. Incapacitated him.

I swallowed the bile that rose in my throat. If I ever found the guy who had hurt Mason, I was going to kill him. I empathized with Justin.

I reached across and gripped one of Mason's hands.

"I think we should call it a day," I said. "Rockford and Justin will still be guilty tomorrow."

Mason turned his head and smiled at me. "You just want me in bed with you again."

"It's possible that's my motive."

"I think I need that right now—your arms around me."

"My arms are all yours. Should we head to my place?"

"Can we go to mine first? I need a change of clothes."

"Sure." I'd only been in Mason's apartment once and it had been an eye-opener. There were things about my lover I didn't understand. He'd explained it had something to do with the bondage being a substitute for shifting into wolf form. Must be like scratching an itch.

I followed him into his apartment. It was exactly as I remembered it, less the row of knives on the kitchen counter.

They'd all been taken into evidence. They'd been clean of any traces.

They were likely just another random obstacle thrown in our path.

While Mason was in his bedroom, I wandered the living room picking up pictures. It looked as if Mason had a happy childhood. There were lots of pictures of a hoard of smiling kids.

I set down a picture of Mason and two older males who might be his parents. It was hard to wrap my head around the fact one of them had birthed Mason. I could see where Mason got his beauty from. Both of his parents, even though they were older, were stunning.

I caught sight of Mason through his open bedroom door. He was undressed down to his briefs. I was drawn to him. I found myself standing in his room, approaching him.

I caught him by the hips and turned him around to face me.

"Hi," I said.

Mason smiled. "Hi back."

"You're beautiful."

Mason looked down.

"Did I say something wrong?" I asked.

"Compliments scare me."

I brushed the back of my hand up Mason's jawline from his chin to his sideburns, then cupped his face. "What the hell did he do to you? What you said earlier about the Rohypnol."

"A few times, he drugged me so I wouldn't object to what he was doing to me."

My stomach dropped.

My sweet Omega. He'd been through so much. The fury I felt was almost blinding. Simply killing Mason's ex would be too good for him. "And the compliments?"

"He'd shower me with them to apologize. Tell me he'd never do it again."

"But he did."

"He would … and he was brutal when he beat me."

I examined Mason's face. His eyebrows had thin scars running through them. I looked from his face to his shoulder, then along to his *claiming area*. There had been a vicious wound there.

I brushed my fingertips across the crescent-shaped, raised marks.

I wanted to hold him in my arms and wipe out every memory of his ex.

"He claimed you."

"As his chosen. Told me I was lucky to find someone who would put up with me."

"He was *so* wrong." I licked my lips and moved closer. "*I* want you."

Mason gripped my face in both hands and crushed his mouth against mine. He shoved me backward, walking me to the edge of the bed. With the back of my thighs against the bed, Mason unbuttoned my shirt and removed it. It landed in a heap on the floor.

My pants were next; undone, he pushed me to lay on the bed. I liked that he was taking charge. I suspected being in control was an unusual thing for him in this room.

He hauled off my shoes and pants. They added to the heap with my shirt.

My cock was hard and weeping when Mason sucked it into his mouth. He slicked it up, bobbing, then used his tongue to play with my slit and my cockhead. He sucked on my tip, clearing the precum, and descended on my cock again.

I jammed one hand into his hair but let him stay in control.

"Up the bed," he said, breaking from my cock. "And flip over."

I scurried up the bed and lay on my stomach.

"Up on your knees," Mason said.

My cock bobbed. I knew where this was going. I'd watched gay porn videos on my computer. I pulled up on my knees, slightly self-conscious that the position exposed my hole.

But that was the whole point.

The bed dipped behind me, and Mason's gentle hands stroked my ass cheeks.

"Are you all right with this?" he asked.

"I'm vibrating, waiting for you to start."

"Impatient." Mason's soft laugh. I quivered as Mason used his thumbs to brush my hole. I closed my eyes, groaning, nearly passing out; the feeling of Mason's tongue was so intense.

He licked and prodded, sending my hole into spasms of desire. Incredible levels of it built in my gut. I pushed my ass back further. Not sure what I expected but I wanted more.

His tongue swirled, his mouth sucking, buried, sending shivers up my spine.

I was sure my cock was dripping precum onto his chic black bedding.

Mason retreated, then one finger was at my entrance.

Yes.

Ever so slowly, he pushed his finger into my body. Once all the way in, he stopped.

"You're wet," he said as he removed his finger.

I wasn't sure why he was telling me this. Yes, it was unusual, but why had it thrown Mason off? I'd pumped my finger into my ass many times. The slickness made it easier.

"Do you remember anything about your father?" Mason asked.

"Just that he was a big guy. But I was a kid, so everyone looked big." I turned and sat on my ass. Mason stared at me. I stared back, my heart thudding. "What's the significance?"

"Humans don't get slick like that, but Alpha male wolves have that level of slickness."

"I'm not a wolf."

"You're a meat eater."

"I also eat salads."

"Have you ever had a crazy squirrely feeling inside you screaming to burst out?"

"I have anxiety sometimes."

Mason lowered his eyes and shook his head.

"Then I don't understand it," he said and crawled toward me. He pushed me over and kissed me. He held my face. "I just know I want you."

I spun us, so I was on top. I linked fingers with him, placed our joined hands to the sides of his head, and descended on his mouth. I ground my cock against him until he sighed and opened his legs. I kissed his chin, then the side of his neck, whining like I'd heard him doing.

It felt good in my throat. Expressed my desperation.

He wrapped his legs around my waist.

"Fill me, Alpha," he whispered. His calling me Alpha this time triggered a different reaction in me. I wanted to protect him and *breed* him with every breath he'd left me with.

I arranged my cock, kissed him, and thrust.

I felt at peace in Mason's warmth. I rolled my hips forward and back, encouraging the most exquisite sounds from him. We were meant to be together. Our attraction had been quick.

Almost fated.

I left his mouth again, headed for an area I was being drawn to. I licked and sucked my way to the claiming area on the side that hadn't been sullied by Mason's ex.

The skin here was pristine.

I ran my tongue across it as I pumped my hips.

"Do it," Mason whispered. "I want to be yours."

Mine.

My heart rate ramped up, pounding in my ears—and my teeth felt as if they were on fire.

Without giving it a second thought, I bit down on Mason's flesh. I tasted blood, so I must have broken his skin. I sucked hard, wanting more. A tingle spread through my mind.

I pulled back when I thought I'd picked up on what Mason was feeling.

"Come back closer," Mason said, clinging to my shoulders. His legs tightened around my waist, his heels riding my ass, and he squeezed as he rocked his hips up.

Incredible pain streaked through my neck and shoulder as his channel clamped down around my cock. Something slipped into place in my mind. He was there. Right there.

He'd bitten me.

It had done something.

I felt connected to him in ways I had never done before.

Exhilarated, I went back to sucking on Mason's claiming area as I thrust my cock into him, my entire world finally making sense. I'd been wandering my entire life, not able to determine which way was up. Now, I had found a partner—a mate.

Mason grunted and met every one of my thrusts.

Fuck.

The base of my cock felt tight. Uncomfortable. It took a bit of effort to press my entire cock into Mason's hole. Then I felt trapped. I had to stop mating with him.

"You've knotted," Mason said. "It'll resolve in a second."

"Like a dog?"

"Like a wolf."

I looked down at his fluttering lashes, seductive green eyes, and perfect lips. I never wanted to look away again. This was me—fulfilled. Nothing else mattered.

"What does it mean?" I asked.

Mason smiled and it melted my heart. "It means you're my Alpha wolf."

"Wolf?"

Mason nodded.

"Fated?"

"I think so."

So many emotions. I couldn't sort through them all. Those were the most incredible words I'd ever heard. That we were fated to be together. That we were a perfect match.

Wolf.

I shook the significance from my mind. I only had one thing more to say. Everything else could wait. "I'm yours, my precious Omega."

Mason hummed with pleasure, sweeping his hands into my hair.

I grunted as the uncomfortable feeling in my cock subsided. I growled, kissed Mason, and pumped into him, flooding his channel with my seed. His body was thirsty for it.

I recovered quickly and we played out the scene two more times.

The sun beginning to set, I lay exhausted beside Mason looking up at the suspension bar. "How do you use that?"

"Cuffs on my ankles. Lower it using that pulley there." He pointed at a chain attached to his ceiling and tied off on one of the walls. "Hook me up, then back up until I'm suspended."

"And you like that?"

"I'm completely at the mercy of who has me up there."

"And what do they do to you up there?"

"Flog me. Use an electric shock rod on my cock. Hang weights off my nipples."

Okay.

Small shiver of excitement at the thought of all that.

"Do you want me to do that to you?" I asked.

Mason rolled onto his side to face me. "I don't need that with you. I'm not trying to forget anything or escape my non-wolf form. I'm present with you. You're all I need."

I sighed, relieved, then remembered—.

We needed to talk about the wolf in the room.

Me.

"Are we saying I'm part wolf shifter?"

"You were drawn to claim me, our minds made a connection, and you knotted."

"Our minds made a connection?"

"Surely, you felt it. Being drawn closer to me."

I hummed and nodded. I'd never felt closer to anyone.

"Do you think my father was a wolf shifter?" I asked.

"It couldn't have been your mother. She was a drug abuser. Most illicit drugs do not affect wolf shifters. It would be impossible to become addicted to them."

"But the Rohypnol? Benedict was likely incapacitated by it."

"I said *most* drugs."

I played with the metal ring on the bedpost, in thought. "If my father was a wolf and my mom wasn't, what does that make me?"

"A half-breed."

"What does that mean?"

"I honestly don't know. It's so rare."

"I've never had any indication I have wolf shifter in my blood."

"My Uncle Jonas' mate Damon, a human, showed no signs of his wolf ancestry other than his sense of smell, his ability to find my uncle, and get him pregnant."

I groaned as my cock pulsed. I wanted to fill Mason with my seed again. An epic-level obsession with doing so. I didn't mind telling him what I was feeling.

"I'm feeling a crazy urge to put a baby in you."

"A pup. It would have to be a pup."

My breathing changed. I gazed into his eyes. They were pure warmth.

"Do you want one?"

Mason rolled onto his back. "That's a big decision."

"You're right. It would be difficult to fit a pup into our lives."

Mason reached for my hand and held it.

"Are we together? Like truly together?" he asked.

"Yes. That whole claiming thing we did … we belong to one another now."

"It was so quick," Mason said.

"If we're fated … of course, it was fast."

"You'll never hurt me?"

I surged up onto my elbow, hovering over Mason. I hoped my expression would relay how sincere I was. "Never, Mason. I will *never* hurt you. I know you believe that already."

Mason nodded. "I do believe that about you, that you're more apt to protect me, but I'm not ready to bring pups into our lives. We barely know each other. I might never be ready."

Mason touched my face. "But I'm on my way to loving you."

My heart skipped so many beats, I thought I was going to go into cardiac arrest. This intelligent, cocky, funny, and beautiful man—wolf had expressed words I'd never heard before. A week ago, I never would have believed any of this would be happening.

I had found my fated mate.

He was falling in love with me.

And me with him.

Mason sat straight up in bed.

"Musty."

"What's musty?"

"I've picked it up several times. At the crime scene. My apartment. Around Justin. And then his sister. I associate that musty smell with pigeons, but what if it's a different bird."

Totally confused.

"I don't understand."

"That falcon that was near my car in the Tennet Technologies parking garage. The rat was a cover tactic. He was spying on us. That's how he got into the suite and my apartment."

"Mason, back up. Where are you going?"

"When I was a young pup, our sire used to read us stories. They were based on history. Told tales about how we were nearly hunted into extinction. We were lucky. We survived."

He paused.

"Other shifters weren't as lucky."

Pretty sure my mouth dropped open. I sat up. "Other shifters?"

"Yeah, foxes, bears … falcons."

"You think Justin is a falcon shifter?"

"It makes sense, doesn't it? Look at him. Those bones. They can barely support his non-falcon form. They're too light. He has to stay that thin."

"It's a long shot. Fantasy realm type stuff."

"One way to find out. Contact the station. See if we have that DNA sample from Justin yet."

"And then what?"

The next step hit me like a brick.

"The feathers at the scene," I said. "We dismissed them as contamination."

"I'll bet you anything those feathers match Justin's DNA," Mason said.

"The small clues Rockford hinted at."

"And we missed them."

"But how did Justin get Benedict in the tub?" I asked.

"He didn't. Rockford did."

"But Justin hates Rockford."

"Not if he thought he was Benedict," Mason replied.

Of course. Benedict must have been sedated, unable to speak by the time Justin appeared on the scene. Rockford pretended to be his brother, lamenting about how much he wanted Rockford dead. And that he finally had his chance to end his miserable brother's life.

Frances had likely told Justin how much Benedict hated Rockford because it was something Justin and Benedict had in common. Justin wanted Rockford dead because of Bryan.

But who *killed* Benedict?

"So, who do you think used the utility knife?" I asked. "And opened his throat."

"If he had someone else to do it … it wouldn't be Rockford. He's too careful. I think if we compare the avian DNA on the utility knife to Justin, we'll get a high probability hit."

"You're right. It wouldn't have occurred to Justin to use gloves. He was counting on the avian DNA throwing us off. He wiped the knife enough to remove his fingerprints."

"But why did he leave the knife behind?" Mason asked.

"Left the suite in falcon form? Couldn't carry it?"

"Then how did he get the knife in there?"

"I don't know," I replied.

"How was he expecting to overpower who he thought was Rockford?"

"Maybe he hadn't thought it through completely."

"And the clothes?" he asked.

"Rockford didn't want to leave any clues behind. He didn't know Justin left the knife."

"Okay," Mason said. "Again."

"Rockford comes back to the suite and finds Benedict there. They share a drink. Rockford drugs Benedict. While he's figuring out what to do next, Justin flies onto the balcony. Rockford convinces him he's Benedict there to kill Rockford. He strips Benedict and drags him to the tub."

Mason picked up where I left off. "Rockford, full of hatred, wants Benedict to bleed out slowly. He fills the tub with ice to bring on hypothermia. Justin cuts Benedict's throat."

"Rockford gathers up all of Benedict's clothes and leaves Justin to tidy up. Justin turns off the bathroom light so who he thinks is Rockford is left to die alone in the dark. Flicks the security bolt on the door. By this time, the hotel staff arrives and knocks on the door."

"How the hell does he manage to break the glass in the sliding door?" Mason asked.

"And what about the boot prints in the soil beneath the balconies."

"We need to bring Justin in for questioning?"

I gathered Mason in my arms and lay back with him. He settled his head on my chest, and I kissed his hair. I inhaled the scent of him and wondered if I was picking up more than a human.

Talk about an existential crisis.

It was possible I was a different species than what I'd assumed this morning.

"Tomorrow, Omega. We'll bring him in tomorrow."

Mason played with the curly hair on my chest.

"Do you need to talk?" he asked. "About the wolf stuff?"

"I need to process first." I tugged Mason closer to me. "I've felt different from the first day I met you. I think you brought out a side of me that might have remained hidden."

"Fated."

"I suppose we should thank Rockford."

Mason snorted. "I'm not thanking him for anything. We would have found each other. We both work in the police department. Our paths would have crossed eventually."

He nuzzled the side of my neck and inhaled.

"I don't detect any wolf on you at all."

"What does a wolf smell like?"

"Like you'd expect. Very much a wet dog smell."

"You don't smell like a wet dog," I said. "You smell like spiced oak."

Mason's body shook as he laughed. "I wear enough cologne to wipe out any wolf smell."

"Why?"

"I don't like other wolves finding me."

"You don't have any wolf friends?"

Mason's fingers danced across my chest, then he made a fist.

"I don't do friends," he said. "Wolf or human."

I looked down at the top of his head. "You don't have any friends?"

"I have eleven siblings. My social interaction bank is forever drained."

"Do you talk to them a lot?"

Mason rolled onto his stomach, crawled toward the edge of the bed, and retrieved his cell phone off his bedside table. "Want to talk to one?"

I surveyed my naked body. "Now?"

Mason plopped down beside me, held the phone over our faces, and dialed one of the numbers in his favorites. *Maddox.* His brother, and the leader of the East Creekside pack.

A face appeared on the screen.

"Mason." A confident smile from a serious but gorgeous face. "Who's this with you?"

Mason snuggled closer to me. "My fated mate, Arnie."

Maddox's eyebrows rose. "You found your fated mate? Adam is going to be thrilled. He worries about you living in the city on your own." He studied me. "Pleasure to meet you, Arnie."

I cleared my throat. This felt so strange talking to Mason's brother while we were in the nude. "Same. Mason has told me a little about Creekside."

Mason adjusted the phone. "How's the family?"

"Growing. There are so many pups around here that we'll be building a new township in the compound to house everyone. You should come home for a visit. Everyone misses you."

"We're in the middle of a murder investigation."

"You work together?"

"We're partners. Just met a few days ago."

"You're not taking the 10 days?"

I clung to Mason's arm. What was Maddox talking about? 10 days to do what?

"We can't," Mason replied. "Things move at a different pace here. We can't take 10 days off to mate." He patted my hand. "We'll be fine. We'll have plenty of time to be together."

"Our protectors will be excited to welcome another pup."

Mason didn't contradict him. His pack expected him to have a pup. Maybe someday he would change his mind. For now, though—I just needed *him*.

"Have you found a mate yet?" Mason asked.

"There's a wolf over in West Creekside I've been seeing. She's a lot of fun."

"I hope things work out."

Maddox nodded. "Time will tell." He looked over his shoulder, then back at us. "I have to go. My Beta has arrived to give me the latest pack update."

"Everything is going well as pack leader?"

"It's a lot of work in addition to the electrical company, but I love it."

"You're made for it."

Maddox smiled. "Thanks. Talk again soon, yeah?"

"I'll keep you up to date."

"Nice to meet you, Arnie. Keep my brother happy, would you? He deserves it."

"It's my life's mission," I said.

Mason closed the call and tossed the phone onto the bed. "I think I want more of that happiness my brother spoke of."

"I don't think that's what he was talking about, but I'm inclined to follow your line of thinking." I stroked his face. "Can we go back to my place, though? I have to feed the cats."

"Damn cats." Mason grinned at me. "As long as I'm with you, it doesn't matter where."

The drive back to my apartment was quick. I might have been speeding. The cats fed, Mason and I hit the sheets. We couldn't get enough of each other. Whatever made us fated mates had kicked into high gear. Exhausted and sore, we finally fell asleep.

When I woke the next morning, tangled up with Mason, my heart soared.

This was where I was supposed to be—with my fated mate in my arms.

Chapter Nine | Mason

I woke to Arnie setting gentle kisses on the back of my head. I had my back plastered to his chest. I hummed and snuggled closer to him. He hugged me tight.

"Good morning," he said, his voice rough.

"Good morning, Alpha."

"Do you think I am … an Alpha?"

"You knotted in me. Only Alpha's can do that, but we could get an ultrasound to find out for certain," I suggested. "Look for a uterus in you."

"I'm not *that* keen to know. I like things the way they are between us."

Me too.

"Any idea what time it is?" I asked.

Arnie rolled away from me and stretched for the bedside table.

"7:30 am."

I groaned. I didn't want to get up, but we needed to interview Justin today. Plus, the results of the search of Bryan and Justin's home would be complete.

Not sure what we were hoping to find.

We managed to have a shower without mating again. I think we both needed a break to recover. The desire was still there but my ass was sore. I'm sure Arnie's cock was too.

The bullpen was busy when we arrived. Everyone had come in early. We were close to solving this. And we all knew it. The results of the DNA test and the search were crucial.

"What do we have this morning?" I addressed the room.

"Justin's DNA profile came back," Linda said.

"Can you have it compared to a DNA profile of the feathers, please?"

Linda's brow furrowed. "Why?"

"I have a theory. Falcon shifters used to populate this area. Justin might be one."

"He can sprout wings?" Linda asked.

"Not exactly," I replied.

"Wait … open mind," an officer said. "We found some unusual clothing at their home."

"What do you mean?" Arnie asked.

The officer held up a shirt still on the hanger. It was a regular shirt, but the sleeves were missing, and the openings for the arms were quite large.

Big enough for wings.

Oh, wow.

Justin wasn't just a shifter; he was able to partially shift.

"The boot prints," Arnie said.

"He was fully dressed when he took off from beneath the balconies," I replied.

"Did we find boots at his place that put him at the scene?"

Linda smiled. "We did. Soil on them matches the soil in the landscaping and on the roof."

"And the boot print?" Arnie asked.

"The tread is a perfect match."

"Sloppy," Arnie said. "I wonder why."

"Not a mastermind like Rockford," I said. "He convinced Justin to leave the knife behind. Told him it was to throw us off. Justin, thinking he was Benedict, believed him. And the trip to my apartment … Rockford suggested that too. He was playing a game. Justin was the pawn."

"Because Rockford hates Justin and wants him to get caught," Arnie said.

"Bryan having a loving relationship with someone other than him infuriates Rockford."

"The obsession has continued," Arnie concluded.

"Can someone please bring Justin in for questioning?"

An officer rose to his feet. "I'll go get him."

"We should bring Rockford in too," I said to Arnie as we headed for my office. "Let him stew in an interview room. Get him good and riled up. Maybe he'll slip."

What the fuck?

I stopped at my doorway and grabbed Arnie's arm, my knees trembling.

On the corner of my desk, a crystal vase with 12 long stem, red roses.

I nearly crumpled to the floor. My heart felt like it stopped. I had to cling to my mate.

Arnie dragged me over to the desk. He picked an enveloped note out of the flowers. I didn't have to guess who the flowers were from. I recognized the handwriting on the envelope.

I needed to sit in my chair. I crawled along the edge of the desk with my hands, Arnie supporting me. I slumped into it. *Blaine Nightingale* had been following me.

He must have seen me go into Arnie's and not come out until this morning.

Arnie opened the note. His face changed, becoming something ugly.

"You don't need to read this," he said.

"Recap it for me."

Arnie's face turned crimson, and he gripped the note tight in his hands. "He still loves you and wants you back. Promises to treat you better. That you're his claimed mate."

I put my hand on my chest. I was having trouble breathing.

All the same words and promises.

"He's going to come for me," I said.

Arnie's features went from ugly to furious. "What do you mean by that?"

"He'll catch me when I'm alone. Play on my emotions—" I hated to say it to Arnie, but it was true. "He'll remind me of the slivers of love that still exist in the depths of my heart."

"You still love him?"

"I've tried to stop, but he's infected me. Sometimes, I still crave his love and approval."

Arnie leaned against my desk. His face … fury—to concern. "What does that mean for us?"

No.

Arnie didn't understand. I rose and went to him. "You're my fated mate. We've claimed each other. Plus, we've connected on a deep level on our own without fate. I believe that."

"Will you be able to fall in love with me?"

I nearly passed out; I became so dizzy. "We're building a love that is all ours."

"But you'll always love him."

I had to take a second. I searched my heart. I held Arnie's face in my hands. I didn't care that my door and blinds were open. "No. Someday, my heart will be filled with love—for you alone."

His face … concern—to relief.

Arnie brought me to him and kissed me. I'd spoken the truth. My heart was starting to beat in unison with my mate's. Fate be damned. This was all us. We were falling in love.

Arnie pulled away. "You're going to be the death of me you're so perfect for me."

"Shut up and kiss me again." A slow descent, then I lost myself in him.

A few dog whistles from the bullpen meant we'd been spotted. Arnie laughed against my lips. "I guess we're busted?"

"It would seem."

I was reluctant to step away from him. I was shaken up, but we needed to go back to being professional. We were detectives in a murder investigation. I took the roses to the break room and dumped them and the vase into the garbage. I flicked the note in on top of it all.

Arnie was right. I didn't need to read it.

I had pure love about to happen in my life. Not like the toxic love I had shared with Blaine; love that was conditional and acted like obsession. I had only received *that* love if I behaved.

I removed a coffee mug from the cupboard and poured a cup of coffee for Arnie. I dressed it the way I had seen him do this morning. The smile I received when I set it on Arnie's desk was worth putting up with the bitter smell of it.

A string of swear words echoed down the hall past the windows of the bullpen. One of my officers had Justin in tow—and our suspect was spitting mad.

"This should be fun," Arnie said, appearing beside me as Justin was ushered into one of the interview rooms. "I've sent someone to retrieve Rockford."

"Excellent. Let's make sure they see each other."

Arnie pulled out his phone and texted someone.

"Let's do this," I said and led the way into a room with a very angry falcon shifter in it.

"You have nothing on me," Justin said.

"Actually, we have a lot on you," Arnie replied.

I turned on the recorder. "Detective Black with Detective Jones interviewing Justin Samson. The time is 0824." I studied

Justin. He wasn't as thin as his sister, but he was still shocking to look at. "Let's start with you having your sister lie for you about your whereabouts on the night of the murder," I said. "If you planned to go to the Grand Metro, you would have been better off going into the city from your house. Your partner wouldn't be asked to testify against you."

"I don't know what you're talking about. I was at my sister's all night."

"According to her, you went out. You went to meet Frances."

"Except Frances never saw you that night," Arnie added.

"I don't know a Frances."

"Then where did you go?"

"No comment." Justin grunted and crossed his arms. "What else have you got?"

"We can place you at the scene. Soil on your boots matches the soil from the landscaping beneath the line of balconies where Rockford frequently stayed."

"So what? Maybe I was standing there, looking up."

"Why would you do that?"

Justin shook his head. "No comment."

"We also found some of that same soil on the roof," I said. "I think you went up there to make it look like someone had rappelled down to Rockford's room."

"And how would I have found my way up there?"

I leaned forward against the desk.

"I'm going to ask you to take off your shirt."

"And if I refuse?"

"We'll have an officer forcibly remove it."

"Am I under arrest? You can't touch me if I'm not under arrest."

Arnie sighed. "Justin Samson you are under arrest for the murder of Benedict Tennet."

I watched Justin's expression as Arnie read him his rights. He was scared. His anger was a cover-up for someone who was panicking. Some parts of his plan had been meticulously thought out. Other parts seemed unplanned. He'd wanted Rockford dead but had left a trail behind. Not sure what would have happened if Rockford hadn't shown up in the suite.

Benedict might still be alive.

Not to play on a pun, but Justin seemed flighty.

"Remove your shirt and turn around," I said. If I were right, Justin's body would have the bulky muscles to support his entire humanoid body in flight.

Justin was slow but he complied.

His bare spine was gruesome looking, a jagged row of square-shaped bumps. And his shoulder blades appeared as protruding plates of bone.

Arnie and I looked at each other in astonishment. Between Justin's shoulder blades and his spine, an incredible display of rippling strength. With those muscles, he could remain in flight for short periods of time. And he was more than strong enough to slam the sliding door too hard.

"It's part of my condition," Justin said as he hauled his shirt back on.

"What condition?" Arnie said. "You being a falcon shifter?"

Justin frowned. "No comment."

"We found avian DNA at the scene."

"Damned pigeons," Justin replied.

"That's what we thought at first, but I suspect your DNA will match the DNA of the feathers we found and the trace evidence on the murder weapon."

"I want my lawyer."

"And who would that be?" I suspected this was going to go full circle.

"Mitchell Dunnigan."

Arnie visibly sighed. "He's not practicing anymore."

Justin laughed. "That's what he likes people to think."

"Pause interview." I stopped the recording. "Jones ... out in the hall, please."

We shut the door on Justin and walked down the hall to the end.

"You think Mitchell was involved after all?" Arnie asked.

"He and Justin both hated Rockford."

"So did Benedict."

"Jeezus, was everyone out to kill Rockford?" I ran my hand through my hair and paced the hallway. "There's no evidence Mitchell was ever in that room."

Arnie let me pace.

"Did we check for evidence on every ice machine in the building?" I asked.

"Impossible to do. We would have had to fingerprint everyone in the hotel. We don't have resources like that. Like you said, we have a budget to adhere to."

"So, Mitchell's fingerprints might be on an ice machine," I said.

"They might be anyway. They were celebrating. Probably having drinks."

"Was Rockford's DNA on the ice machine on their floor?"

Arnie shook his head. "Couldn't isolate it. Too many people have touched the machine."

"And Mitchell's hands aren't big enough to make the bruises on Benedict's arms."

"Nope."

"No hair fibres—nothing?"

"Mason ... it's a hotel room. There are likely hundreds of hair samples in there."

"So, Justin lured Mitchell there to throw us off," I said. "We're going with that?"

"Justin must have sought Mitchell out; retained him as a lawyer for who knows what. Found out Mitchell lost his job because of that Rockford case."

"How? Justin isn't exactly ringing the high intelligence bells."

Arnie rolled his eyes. "I bet you Mitchell knows Frances."

"She told Justin about Mitchell?" I sighed. "Yeah, that fits."

"You go back in with Justin. I'll give Frances a call."

I returned to the interview room. Justin had his head down on his folded arms on the table. I slammed the door. His head popped up.

"Did you call my lawyer?"

"We have one more thing to check first." I leaned back and crossed my arms.

And waited.

The lack of progress flustered Justin enough that he started making little noises. Not going to say I knew them to be bird noises, but I suspected they were.

Arnie let himself into the room and set a piece of paper in front of me.

It simply said, *yes*.

Frances *did* know Mitchell. She was a talker; exactly what Justin needed. It seemed she'd told Justin that Benedict hated Rockford enough that she was worried about Rockford's safety. She'd told Justin how frequently Rockford stayed in the suite. And that Rockford had lost Mitchell his job … and when Mitchell's anniversary was. She'd inadvertently served Justin well.

I turned on the recorder. "Resuming the interview with Justin Samson. Time 0931."

"We know you're friends with Frances," Arnie said.

"No comment."

"Your boot prints show evidence that you took off from there. Heavy pressure on the toes."

"No comment."

Arnie's phone buzzed. He looked down at it, then stood up, and opened the door. A few seconds later, one of my officers paraded Rockford past the doorway. He made sure to stop so Rockford would see Justin sitting in the interview room.

I saw panic register in Rockford's eyes.

In his mind, avian DNA shouldn't have led us to Justin. His little game had gone wrong. Hinting at the bird feathers at the scene was meant to annoy us—not help us.

I moved my attention back to Justin. Seeing Rockford had him fuming. He was starting to piece things together. That if, on a long shot, we were successful in solving the case, the finger would be pointed at him, not Rockford. That Rockford had set him up.

Justin had been way too easy to play.

A part of me felt sorry for him.

Linda came into the room, cleared her throat, and set a paper in front of me.

I scanned it and then passed it to Arnie.

"Okay, Justin," I said. "We can place you at the scene. Your DNA is all over it."

Justin glared at me. "Doesn't mean I killed him."

"So, you admit you were there," Arnie said.

"I wanted to talk to him," Justin replied.

"You flew up there?" I asked.

Justin leaned forward; his face twisted in pain. Before our eyes, his arms became grey and white wings. A falcon's. He fluttered them a few times, then tucked them at his side.

"So what?" he said. "I wanted to surprise him."

"To kill him," Arnie said.

"To talk to him. Tell him to stop bothering Bryan."

My stomach churned, remembering the flowers on my desk.

"Rockford was in contact with Bryan?" I asked.

"Sitting outside in his car," Justin said, "watching the house. Deliveries of flowers. Notes and cards in the mail. Even showed up at the door a few times."

"He was wearing Bryan down?" Arnie asked.

"A few weeks ago, Bryan wanted to meet Rockford for coffee … to talk."

"That gives you motive to murder Rockford, Justin. You do realize that."

"Did he meet him?" I asked.

Justin nodded.

"You were afraid of losing Bryan."

Tears collected in Justin's eyes. "I love him *so* much."

I was convinced Justin was the one who made the cut that ended Benedict's life.

"Why did Rockford take Benedict's clothes?" I asked.

Justin stared at me, eyes wide, his breathing becoming rapid. "You *know* he was there?"

"Bruises we found on Benedict's arms prove he was dragged to that tub. The impressions do not match the size of your fingers even though, I suspect, you're strong enough to do it."

"It was his idea," Justin blurted out. "I came to scare Rockford. Frances said he would be there. When I arrived, the wolf I thought was Benedict was standing over his incapacitated brother. He'd already stripped him and started to fill the tub with ice."

"Rockford dragged Benedict to the tub and continued filling it with ice," Arnie said.

"But you made the cut that ended Benedict's life," I added. "Who brought the utility blade in? Was that you? Were you wearing a pouch with the knife in it?"

Justin shook his head. "No comment."

"Your DNA is on the murder weapon, Justin."

Justin sighed and slumped his feathered shoulders. "I thought I was killing Rockford."

"And after you killed Benedict, Rockford convinced you to wipe your prints off the weapon but leave it behind," Arnie said. "You didn't think to question that?"

Justin wrinkled his brow as he looked at Arnie. "Of course, I questioned it."

"But you decided to believe him."

Justin's bottom jaw jutted out. "He wasn't the one who convinced me."

What?

I moved forward to the edge of my seat.

"Who did?" I asked.

Justin swallowed and ruffled his wings. "Frances."

Jeezus.

We hadn't even considered that. That Frances was involved. She had direct communication with the Grand Metro. She would have known when Rockford and Benedict were staying there. She could have orchestrated the murder. Of *Benedict*. Worked with Rockford to set it up.

"Was she there in the room?" Arnie asked.

Justin nodded.

"She wanted to see Benedict die?" I added.

"She made sure not to touch anything," Justin said. "I was surprised to see her. She *wasn't* surprised to see me. She was the one who told me Rockford would be alone in the suite that night. That the concierge guy who Rockford was having sex with would have been and gone."

"She encouraged you to make it *that* night you visited him," Arnie said.

"She said it was a golden opportunity."

"And then convinced you to leave the murder weapon behind and deliver that glass to Detective Black's home and arrange the knives to confuse us."

"It was Rockford's idea. Frances went along with it." Justin frowned. "She must have known it was Benedict in the tub. She trusted Rockford's prowess when it came to crimes."

"And you trusted her," I said.

"I've known her since college."

"Did she have a reason for wanting Benedict dead?"

Justin tipped his head to one side. "Frances is certifiable crazy. She kept making sexual advances toward Benedict and he kept turning her down."

"Because he was into males," I said.

"She figured that out. I was shocked when she told me she'd seen men coming and going from his house. It was next level, the fact she was stalking him."

"Who took the clothes?"

"Frances. When she left, she had his clothes gathered in her arms, sniffing them. It was creepy and it was confusing. I couldn't understand why she would want Rockford's clothes. I figured his scent might be the same as Benedict's. She wanted that scent to take home."

I looked at Arnie. He started typing on his notepad.

A search warrant for Frances' home.

I reached for the recorder. "Stop interview. Time 0957."

Arnie called an officer into the interview room. He would have Justin write down his statement, then take him down to the jail. He wouldn't be seeing freedom for a very long time.

We turned our attention to Rockford in the next room.

After starting the recorder, Arnie, and I both just stared at him for a few minutes. We needed Rockford to be annoyed. Annoyed and worried Justin had spilled.

"We can place you at the scene," Arnie said at last.

"How?"

"Justin told us you were there," I replied.

"He hates me. Of course, he'd lie about me being there."

"Why does he hate you?"

"Because Bryan is mine." He leaned forward. "Bryan is confused. He knows he wants to be with me. We're destined to be together. I just need to remind him that he loves me."

"You've been trying," Arnie said. "And it's not working. Have you ever considered that Bryan has moved on and is in love with Justin?"

Rockford sneered. "I suspect Justin is out of the picture now."

I almost threw up. I'd already been feeling queasy, but the thought of Rockford moving in on Bryan now that Justin was going to prison stirred up a feeling of disgust and personal fear.

I hoped Bryan was strong enough to resist him because it was unlikely we'd be able to put Rockford behind bars. All we had was Justin's testimony. Rockford was right; Justin hated Rockford enough to place him at the scene of a murder he had committed.

A judge would throw that evidence out.

"We have impressions of your fingers on Benedict's body," I said.

Rockford leaned back in his chair. "Prove it."

"We have two glasses, both with the same DNA on them. You were in that suite."

"My brother was a lush. Was probably two-fisting it."

That didn't even make sense. The bottle had been right there on the table.

"The neighbors heard a conversation before the ice machine started going."

"Maybe my brother was watching television."

This was pointless. Rockford had an answer for everything and there was no way he was going to crack and admit to being there. Why would he? We had no proof.

"Stopping interview." I stopped the recording.

"I have a question," I said.

"Shoot," Rockford replied.

"What did you do to get written out of your parents' will?"

Rockford sneered. The action gave me full body chills.

"Dearest Mother had a best friend … Betty. And Betty had the most beautiful son."

I gripped the edge of the table until my fingers hurt.

"Sweet sixteen," Rockford continued. "So innocent."

I jumped to my feet so fast, my chair flew back. "Stop!"

Arnie leaped up and burst around the table. "Get out of here!"

Rockford smirked. "Have a lovely day."

Watching that piece of shit walk out through the doors at the end of the hall was beyond infuriating, but at least we had our murderer. I gripped Arnie's sleeve. I felt sick. It shouldn't have surprised me that Rockford would be capable of more than domestic abuse.

"Breathe, Omega. It's not over yet."

"I was hoping to get him as an accessory to murder."

"There's still time to nail that son of a bitch to the wall."

"How?"

Arnie looked at his notepad. "Search warrant for Frances' home came through. Do we want to attend? They might be awhile. Would it help if you ate something?"

My stomach grumbled, but I also felt dizzy. I wasn't sure I could keep anything down. No sooner had I thought it, than I had to dash for the bathroom to throw up.

The flowers from Blaine and Rockford's implied confession had really upset me. My whole body was reacting. I only managed a string of dry retching. I had nothing in my stomach.

"Are you all right?" Arnie stepped into the cubicle behind me. I hadn't even had enough time to lock it. I clung to the toilet seat. His gentle hand came to rest on my back.

"Rockford plus those flowers have my stomach tied in knots," I said.

"I'm not going to leave your side. Your ex won't be able to get to you."

I laughed softly. "You're going to be sick of me."

Arnie rubbed small circles on my back. "Never."

I gripped the toilet seat as the room spun. "I really don't feel well."

"Do I need to take you home?"

"We need to be here for the results of Frances' search."

"Well, let's get you to your office at least."

I made it there under my own steam, but I kept a tight grip on Arnie's sleeve. After I sat at my desk, Arnie left and fetched me a glass of water. I finished drinking the whole thing.

My mate looked worried.

"I'm all right," I said. "Just a bit stressed out."

"I won't let him hurt you. I'm your fated mate."

The room spun.

Oh, my God.

I gripped the desk, a heat wave of panic striking me. "Hand me the garbage can."

Arnie was quick to bring it to me. My entire stomach full of water ended up in it.

Linda leaned against my doorframe. "We found something in the search already."

I used the back of my hand to wipe my face. "What?"

"A man's suit. The only one in the entire apartment. It was in Frances' bed."

"Oh, wow," Arnie said. "Tell forensics to hustle on the DNA profile on it."

"We have her," I said after Linda left. "She had something to do with the murder."

I placed my head in my hand and leaned my elbow on the desk.

So dizzy.

A memory of Adam nauseated and throwing up circulated through my mind. I'd seen it many times while I'd been growing up. Having 12 pups came with a lot of morning sickness.

My heart did a little shudder.

I was on birth control.

No.

I had another memory. My sire and Adam joking about how useless birth control was in the prevention of pregnancy in Adam. I reached for Arnie. He took my hand.

It had only been a couple of days since we'd started mating.

But deep down, I knew the truth.

I squeezed Arnie's hand and gazed into his serene brown eyes.

"I think I'm pregnant."

Arnie looked confused. "You're on birth control."

"Family history of it being unreliable."

Arnie came closer and wrapped his arms around my head, my cheek on his chest. I closed my eyes as he kissed my head. This was so far out of where I had seen my life going.

I'd thought I'd be alone forever.

"Are you happy about it?" Arnie asked, his chest rumbling beneath my face.

"I'm going to be honest with you. I don't know yet. The news is seconds old."

"Is it all right for me to be happy?"

I smiled against his shirt. "Of course."

"We could make it work … pups."

Maybe.

It hurt my heart to say the words, "Let's finish this case before we talk about it." I looked up at him. "Okay? I have some soul-searching to do."

Arnie stroked my cheek with his fingers. "Whatever you decide to do, I'm here. I'm not going anywhere. You don't need to worry about losing me."

I nodded and went back to finding comfort against his shirt, surrounded by his scent.

Linda poked her head in again. "We have Frances here. She went off when we arrived at her home with the search warrant. Assaulted one of the officers when they tried to detain her."

"Is she in an interview room?"

"At the end of the hall."

"You all right to do this?" Arnie asked me.

"My stomach feels like it might give me a break. I should be fine."

I was able to walk to the interview room without clinging to Arnie. I refocused, locking onto the details of the case. Contemplating my desire to carry a pup or not would have to wait.

Frances was handcuffed to the table.

I started the recorder.

"Why the clothes, Frances?" Arnie asked. "Were you that obsessed with Benedict? Because you knew it was Benedict who was being murdered that night, didn't you?"

"I didn't kill him," she said.

"Never said you did," I replied. "But you were there, weren't you?"

"He wouldn't even look at me."

"Benedict?"

"At least Rockford paid attention to me … for a while."

I shivered. Rockford was pervasive.

"When did he stop paying attention to you? Rockford." Arnie asked.

Frances pursed her lips. "When he took over at Tennet Technologies."

"After the murder."

"Yes."

"Any idea why that would be? That he would lose interest in you."

"Because he's just like his brother. Only interested in cock."

"And that makes you mad?" I asked.

"Doesn't make me happy, that's for sure."

"Upset enough to partake in a murder?"

"I can place him there," Frances said.

"Who?"

"Rockford."

"You saw him there?"

"I knew they'd both be there. I wanted to make sure nothing untoward happened."

Arnie shook his head. "I don't believe you. I think you planned the whole thing with Rockford. To kill his brother. And you brought Justin in to take the fall for the murder."

"Rubbish," Frances said. "I didn't want Benedict dead. I loved him."

"A love he didn't return," I said. "And never would. You didn't want anyone else to have him, did you? All those men you saw coming and going to Benedict's house made you livid."

Someone knocked on the door.

I opened it to Linda. She handed me an evidence bag with a small vile in it.

"Found it in the pocket of the suit jacket Frances had in her bed," she whispered.

"Does it contain Rohypnol?"

"Affirmative."

"Thank you." I closed the door.

"The suit in your bed … it belongs to Benedict, doesn't it? You wanted it to remember him by." I held up the evidence bag. "Did you slip this into the pocket or did Rockford?"

Frances gripped the edge of the table, her eyes wide.

Rockford.

Throwing doubt on his tracks again. He had probably suggested that Frances take the suit.

"Tell us why you were really there," Arnie said.

"Will it be enough to put Rockford away if I tell you?"

"That's possible. Were you using the office phone to talk to him about killing Benedict?"

"Sometimes."

Frances might not be aware, but businesses the size of Tennet Technologies made a habit of recording all incoming and outgoing calls on their lines. They did it to protect themselves.

"There will be recordings of those calls leading up to the murder."

"There will?"

I nodded.

Frances released a long sigh. "The suit belonged to Benedict. I took it from the suite after Rockford suggested I should ... as a keepsake."

"And you told him Benedict would be there."

"I tracked Benedict there many times. He was like clockwork when he stayed in that room. It might have been pure chance Rockford didn't show up at the same time, except he had his own schedule. His visits didn't intersect with Benedict's. I was able to determine who was who."

"And Justin was always intended to be the one caught for murder."

"He turned me down in college and then he met *that* Bryan."

I almost rolled my eyes.

Femme Fatale.

"Thought we'd make it puzzling for you, Rockford and I."

"Were you there when he hauled Benedict into the tub?"

"I stayed until Justin cut his throat. Let Benedict see me as the blood drained from him."

Arnie rose to his feet. "Frances Littleton, I am placing you under arrest as an accessory to the murder of Benedict Tennet ...."

We had enough to arrest and charge Rockford. Two people had placed him at the scene. We would have phone records of the conversations between him and Frances. Even if she used her cell phone, we'd be able to request transcripts of the calls. We had them both.

Rockford's streak had come to an end. He'd tripped up.

I had one last question.

"Why did you recommend Mitchell Dunnigan to Justin as a lawyer?"

Frances smiled. "I thought it would be funny given Mitchell's history with Rockford."

"Let's go." Arnie cuffed both her wrists and hustled her out of the room. I was confident we would verify the suit found in Frances' apartment belonged to Benedict. The team would organize all our findings into cases against Rockford, Justin, and Frances.

I could take a minute … and consider my own life.

In all likelihood, I was expecting a pup. *We* were expecting a pup. My fated mate and me. If Adam met Arnie, he would say Arnie was everything I deserved and more.

Maybe he was right.

Maybe I deserved happiness.

"Omega?"

I whipped around in my chair. Standing in the doorway, the love that had nearly destroyed my life. Blaine Nightingale.

"How the hell did you get in here?"

"You forget, I know my way around back here."

My breath faltered. When I was still an officer, I'd taken him into these back rooms and rutted with him on more than one occasion late at night.

"You shouldn't be here."

"I needed to see you." He took a step toward me, and I recoiled. "Don't be like that. You know we're meant to be together. I still love you. I'm willing to take you back."

"I've found my fated mate."

Blaine laughed. "Who?" He hitched his thumb over his shoulder. "That human?"

"He's not human."

"Even if he's not, he can't take care of you like I can. You know that."

"He's my Alpha. We've claimed one another."

"None of that matters. You know you still love me. Do you love *him*?"

I dragged my breath in and out, my heart thumping violently around in my chest. I would not be telling Blaine before I'd even told Arnie.

A second figure created a shadow in the doorway. One much bigger than Blaine. My ex jumped forward as a thundering growl permeated the room around us.

My very soul filled with pride.

And love.

My Arnie.

My Alpha. His impressive canines had descended, and his face had changed enough to amplify the growl followed by a snarl as his hands descended on Blaine's shoulders.

Given the opportunity, he might have shifted.

Instead, he ripped Blaine from the room.

Arnie wouldn't be undisciplined enough to kill Blaine, but I suspected, I would never be bothered by my abuser again. Arnie would put the fear of death in him.

When Arnie finally returned, his canines were showing over his bottom lip. I rushed to him and put my hands on his face. I ran my thumbs down his fangs, root to tip.

"So sexy," I said and smiled.

Arnie placed his hands on mine. "I love you."

Tears collected in my eyes. I'd never said it before and truly meant it. This time, my whole heart and soul knew it to be true—and absolute.

I gazed into his eyes as I brushed my lips across his.

"I love you too."

It felt like a weight lifted off my shoulders.

There it was.

Hope.

Chapter Ten | Arnie

We'd finished packing away the last of the bondage gear. The pulley had been a bit of a chore. I wasn't an expert in home repairs, and we had to borrow a ladder from the building manager.

Mason wasn't allowed anywhere near ladders.

He had precious cargo on board.

Five weeks since he'd told me he was pregnant; Mason's belly was round and firm. I spent a lot of time talking against his stretched skin. And to make Mason giggle—singing.

I wanted our pup to know both of our voices.

And it was a pup. An early ultrasound had confirmed we were going to be having a furry bundle. That meant our pup would be a shifter.

Unlike me.

We'd tried. The most I could muster was descended canines, long nails, and an extended mishappened muzzle. Mason loved my canines on his skin, teasing his flesh.

I moved in two weeks ago. It had been difficult leaving the apartment I'd grown up in, but we'd agreed, Mason's apartment was in a better neighborhood. We wanted somewhere safe for our pup to grow up. With two detective salaries, we might even be able to afford something better. For now, though, we were happy to start our lives together in Mason's apartment.

I came up behind Mason and gathered him in my arms and kissed the back of his neck.

"Sweet Omega," I grumbled against his skin.

"Alpha." He turned to face me and threaded his fingers into my hair. Having his lips so close to mine always made my stomach tumble and flip; I loved him so much.

Mason brought me closer and pulled my lips to his, a low moan released by him filling my throat. The pregnancy had made Mason more than amorous.

I kept my lips on him as long as I could while I collected the material of his shirt in my hands. I relinquished his mouth and pulled his shirt off over his head.

Our pace increased as we stripped off our clothes and cascaded onto the bed, a tumble of exploring hands and devouring lips. Our growing desire for one another was frantic enough to leave me breathless. I trapped Mason on the bed, straddling his thighs, and pinned his hands.

His emerald eyes were alight with lust.

And love.

I kissed him slowly as I moved his hands above his head. He would keep them there for me, draped atop his head. He groaned and thrust his hips up as I moved my lips to his neck.

I dragged my stubble along his skin, making him shiver, and tugged on his warm thick earlobe with my teeth. I had full control over my canines now. I wasn't using them today.

Today, I had other ideas.

I drew a damp line with my tongue from behind his ear, down his neck, to his clavicles. I sucked on one, making Mason squirm. He sighed my name.

I sat up and looked down at him. He was the most gorgeous being I had ever set eyes on. Fluttering lashes—lips parted, tongue darting out and in. I shuffled further down his legs.

My gaze traveled from his eyes to his lips to his jutted chin. And down his throat. I groaned with desire as I caressed his nipples with my thumbs. They were thick, puffy, and leaking.

I gathered one in my mouth—and sucked, the milk spraying the back of my throat. Mason swore and thrust his chest up. I circled his nipple with my tongue as I cupped his soft pecs. I moved my attention from one nipple to the other. The gift from his body filled my mouth.

I set a milky kiss on his sternum.

Mason mewled beneath me, his hard cock jumping against my abs.

I kissed the crest of his swollen belly, then sucked and licked my way to his distended naval. I held his belly in my hands as I hummed against it. Lower—I kissed his skin and wrapped my hand around his cock, pumping it slowly. The angle would be awkward, but I could get in there, the daily shrinking space between his belly and his thighs.

Mason's cock was tight and straining as I sucked him into my mouth.

I adjusted my position, coming at him at a right angle, my feet hanging off the side of the bed, my head in his lap. I held his belly away from my face with one hand, sucking and slurping on his cock, my head bobbing. I reached through, cupped his sacs, and played with his hole.

It pulsed and jumped beneath my touch.

Mason's legs tensed, and he jammed his hips up. I had to adjust to keep his cock in my mouth. I slipped up and down his length with my lips, my tongue caressing.

I pressed my finger into his soaking wet hole.

Mason unleashed down my throat, coming completely undone. It took a while for his body to stop jerking and pulsing. He shuddered, coming down off his last release.

I slipped his cock from my mouth and went to join him on the pillows. He found *his spot* on my chest, his hair against my chin, his hand playing with my chest hair.

"Three more weeks," Mason said.

"We're almost there."

"I wonder what color the pup will be."

"Could be anything. We don't know the color of mine or my sire's fur." I kissed his head. "I'm hoping our pup is grey like you, with those adorable patches of white at your muzzle."

Mason had been shifting in the apartment frequently. The effect of his swollen belly made sleep difficult. As soon as we returned home from work, he would take a *wolf nap*.

After taking an antihistamine, I often stroked his furry head until he fell asleep.

"Are we ready for this?" Mason asked.

"We have the nursery all set up."

Mason shook his head. "No, I meant, are *we* ready for this?"

I knew what he meant. Our relationship was still so new.

"Mason, I adore you beyond what I thought a soul was capable of loving. We're going to bring this pup into a home filled with so much love. That's as ready as we need to be."

Mason snuggled closer. "You're my one and only love."

My mate had stopped waking up in the middle of the night, on the verge of screaming. The hold his abuser had on him over time vanquished to a dull roar. I knew there would always be that small sliver of fear in Mason's heart, but he had found safety and compassion in my arms.

He slung his leg over my thigh and arranged his belly against my side. I smiled. I was his own personal body pillow. I closed my eyes and inhaled the scent of him. I knew it intimately now, his scent. I could recall it in my mind when I was away from him. I knew when he entered a room; could detect the subtle change when he was upset or aroused.

"Love you," he mumbled against my chest.

I breathed up into those words.

And locked them in my heart.

This is what true love felt like. This was beyond fate.

My Omega.

My Mason.

"I love you too."

I fell asleep dreaming of him, our pup, and our life together.

I just needed to meet his family first.

Epilogue

Mason was right. Creekside Township *was* sleepy. Main Street was practically empty aside from a few cars parked outside a grocery store and a restaurant called *Growlers* that Mason told me belonged to his Uncle Jonas; his mate owned *Creekside Delicatessen* across the street.

After driving through town, we traveled into the surrounding hills. I held tight to little Lucas as we bumped our way up a long gravel driveway. Our pup had reached his 6-week milestone. We'd begun supplementing his voracious milk consumption with a meat mash.

"Wow," Mason said as he slowed at the top of the driveway. "Maddox wasn't kidding."

"What?"

"There were only five houses up here when I left."

I counted the houses. I could see eleven. My stomach did a nervous flip. I was about to find myself among an entire pack of wolves. I brought Lucas to my nose and sniffed him.

He smelled incredible.

The scent of him settled my anxiety. Mason had told me it was because Lucas was an Alpha; my body was reacting to Lucas' ability to someday stand by my side as a protector.

Doors opened up and down the collection of houses, and a multitude of people made their way toward our truck. Mason pulled off the driveway and parked. "You ready for this?"

"Don't leave me alone for a single second."

Mason smiled at me and patted my thigh. "You're going to love them."

It wasn't like I didn't know many of them. Mason spoke to at least two of his siblings, cousins, and protectors every week. He frequently invited me into the conversations.

I'd grown quite fond of Adam, Mason's carrier. I could see a lot of Mason in Adam. How his voice could become so soft and caring, and the way he held his mouth, and wrinkled his nose.

His protectors, Adam and Lucas were the first to reach the truck.

What looked to be at least 40 wolves surrounded us, accompanied by a swarm of furry pups running in and out of their feet. I passed little Lucas to Mason's sire, Lucas Sr.

He sniffed our pup and passed him to Adam.

Sniff—pass. Sniff—pass. Until our Lucas had made the rounds of the entire pack. Mason had warned me the pack would do that, so they could learn his scent.

I was glad to have him back in my hands.

The gorgeous wolf I knew to be Maddox stepped closer to us. "We've planned a hunt in honor of you coming back to us for a visit."

Mason rocked from foot to foot. "Maddox, I haven't hunted since I was sixteen."

"Then you'll be glad to get out there and run through the trees."

Mason bit his bottom lip and looked at me. "Do you mind? I'd need to leave you here."

I couldn't imagine anything more enjoyable for Mason than running free through the forest in wolf form. I knew it was hard on him only shifting in the privacy of our apartment.

Afterward, I had something I wanted to ask him.

Adam leaned against me. "We have plenty of nursing wolves to keep little Lucas fed." He petted Lucas's head with his fingertips. "They could be gone a while."

I smiled at Mason and nodded. Moments later, I stood on the front porch of a massive log home and watched as over 20 wolves stripped off their clothes and shifted: a writhing mass of skin and fur. The crunching sound coming from them was nauseating.

Shifted, Mason ran up the steps and nudged my leg with his nose.

I petted his head. "We'll be all right. Adam is going to take care of us."

Mason blinked at me, turned his head, and trotted down the stairs, joining the group of wolves as they ran for the trees. This was going to be good for him. I couldn't imagine having the need to hunt ingrained in my bones, and not being able to do it.

"Shall we head inside?" Adam asked and opened the door. "This is Maddox's house now, but it's quieter than ours. Many of our pups and their families live with Lucas and me."

"I like that your family is so close."

"They're just glad of the built-in pup sitter." Adam settled in an armchair and motioned for me to hand him Lucas. It felt strange handing our pup over to someone. The *sniff and pass* had almost given me a heart attack. It was possible Mason, and I were overprotective parents.

We'd both taken time off work since Lucas was born, not wanting him out of our sight. Our vacation time was running out. We knew we'd need to return to our detective duties soon.

But not yet.

Adam hummed on the top of Lucas' little head and kissed him.

I relaxed. Our pup was in safe hands.

The next few hours passed with easy conversation. A young male wolf came in halfway through and fed Lucas. He was the son of a Mark and Reese Cooper.

Mason had drawn a chart including every wolf in his pack on a piece of butcher paper. It was the only material large enough. I was most interested in *his* family. When he spoke of them, Mason's face lit up. I loved to see him smiling. Slowly, over time, he'd been doing it more.

"Here they come," Adam said and stood. "They have four deer."

"What happens next?"

"Maddox and some of his siblings will dress them. We can cook some of the meat for you."

"Appreciated."

My Mason come stumbling through the front door, nude, and laughing, his face covered in blood. Other than whelping Lucas, this was the happiest I had ever seen him.

"Alpha!" He ran at me, wrapped his arms around my neck, and kissed me. I'd become accustomed to the taste of blood on his lips, often kissing him after he'd finished feeding.

The fangs turned me on.

The blood didn't bother me.

My stomach flipped, my nerves reminding me of what I had planned.

"Get your clothes," I said to him. "Lucas and I have something we want to ask you."

Mason stepped back and tipped his head to one side. "Intriguing."

I followed Mason down the front steps, Lucas cupped in my hands. Mason found his clothes and dressed himself. I waited impatiently as he pulled on his boots and tied them.

"Okay," he said. "What do you want to ask me?"

"Lucas and I want to ask you."

Mason smiled. "Okay, Lucas and you."

"Can we head for the trees? I want to be away from everyone."

Mason cocked an eyebrow at me. "Cryptic. I love it." He led the way across the field and into a small stand of trees. We were hidden from the view of the houses.

I kissed Lucas on the head for courage … and got down on one knee. I set him on the ground at my feet. He'd be fine for a few moments.

I looked up and Mason was staring at me, his lips parted. "Arnie …?"

"I know it's a human custom …." I dug around in my pocket, produced a ring, and held it out toward him. "But I want the whole world to know how much I love you. Wolf and human."

Tears rimmed Mason's gorgeous emerald eyes … and he nodded.

My heart fluttered and I felt faint. "Is that a *yes*?"

Mason dropped to his knees and grasped my hands. "Of course, it's a *yes*. I love you, the wolf and human of you, and I will marry you a thousand times over Arnold Jones."

There was so much love in the gaze he held me captive in. I could live a thousand of those lifetimes of marriages and never find the end of my love for him.

Lucas squeaked and let out his first bark.

Mason and I beamed at each other, laughing.

My mate often spoke of hope and how I had brought it into his life.

I felt it in my soul as we kissed.

Hope.

The lone wolf who had run from me on the first day was no longer alone.

We had each other.

For all time.

About the Author

JT Fader is an alternate pen name for Leigh Jarrett (she/he), allowing Leigh to explore their love of MM+ paranormal and fantasy stories by creating their own worlds.

In their hometown of Victoria, BC, Canada, Leigh can be found nestled up with their fabulously supportive wife and trusty laptop or enjoying the wondrous Vancouver Island outdoors.

To stay up to date with JT Fader's new releases and promos, check out their JT Fader Fantasticals website at www.jtfader.com.

You can also find Leigh on Bluesky.